Pick Up

Pick Up

J. A. O'Brien

ROBERT HALE · LONDON

© James O'Brien 2008
First published in Great Britain 2008

ISBN 978-0-7090-8503-4

Robert Hale Limited
Clerkenwell House
Clerkenwell Green
London EC1R 0HT

www.halebooks.com

2 4 6 8 10 9 7 5 3 1

Typeset in 11¾/15pt Palatino
by Derek Doyle & Associates, Shaw Heath
Printed and bound in Great Britain
by Biddles Limited, King's Lynn

Dedicated to my wife Anna, my best friend, with love

CHAPTER ONE

Tense and preoccupied, Jack Carver came out of the blind corner and thought there was no chance of avoiding the hitch-hiker. Instinct kicked in and he veered away. As he flashed past the woman he was thankful that only a couple of days previously he had fitted new tyres to the Vectra. It was the second day of an almost continuous downpour. Surface water, added to the late August greasiness at the end of a heavenly summer would have seen him, had he not had new tyres, plunge into the dyke at the far side of the road, or worse, into one of the stout oaks lining the road. Surface water drenched the woman. As he zigzagged away, Carver recalled an elphin face with a blond fringe poking out from under the hood of a yellow jacket like the high visibility attire worn by police and emergency services personnel.

His preoccupation had to do with the company conference to which he was on his way. He had a lot of ground to make up. The building society of which he was branch manager in Loston had recently opened a new branch; the launch had become a PR fiasco when Graham Williams, whose apartment he had repossessed a couple of weeks previously, had shown up ranting and raving. And when he was joined by a woman called Imelda Bell, the sister of one Lucy Bell, a long-serving employee whom he had recently dismissed, equally vociferous in her condemnation of him, what had been a low-key middle-page press item had become a front-page scoop. To add to his woes, the officers in a passing police car had intervened.

The opening had become a circus. And the ringmaster, Julius Roycroft, the recently appointed CEO, had not been pleased when he had to intervene to prevent both protesters from being arrested. 'Bloody lousy timing, Carver,' had been his scowling rebuke. 'Public sympathy is always with the dispossessed. And that's the stuff of a first-day tutorial. This kind of cock-up we do not need!'

Careerwise, it had not been a good day for Jack Carver. Talk about a move to head office had dried up. And to heap trouble on trouble, he had just lived through a week of hell when financial irregularities had been highlighted in a surprise audit. The fact that a computer glitch had been responsible did nothing to restore his standing. Another problem was Mattie (Matilda) Clark, a ticking time bomb which he was not at all confident of being able to defuse, a mistress wanting to become a permanent nester.

Hence the pounding migraine and tense neck muscles.

A short distance on he came to a pub. He was about to go past, but on impulse he turned in. Brigham, where the conference was being held was only thirty miles from Loston, but he felt in need of a break. A flash of headlights and a blaring horn alerted him to how close he had come to becoming a statistic. A white Almera flashed past, followed by a black Ka.

The pub was empty except for an elderly man sitting at the bar nursing a pint of bitter, and a man reading a tabloid newspaper sitting nearer the door.

'Coffee,' he requested of the bored barmaid.

'A miserable one, eh,' said the old duffer who, uninvited, joined Carver.

'Bloody awful,' Carver agreed. 'If it keeps coming down like this it'll be a boat and not a car I'll need.'

'Sorry.' The old duffer readjusted an ancient hearing aid. 'Say again.' Carver felt uncomfortable under the man's concentrated fixation on his mouth. Obviously attempted lip-reading became essential when the hearing aid acted up.

'I said . . .'

The lights dipped.

'Lightning about,' the old duffer said.

Carver took his coffee, went and sat some way off, not wanting the bother. His thoughts again turned to Mattie Clark. He had met Clark at a company meeting three years previously and had immediately fallen into bed with her, still not sure whether he was the hunter or the hunted, the seducer or the seduced. Since that first tryst there had been repeat performances. However, unexpectedly Mattie Clark's mood had changed. She had shed her good time girl attitude to their relationship and had become proprietorial. 'You just can't shag me and then return to the little woman all the time,' had been her angry outburst the last time they had met, when he had reminded her, foolishly so in retrospect, of their no ties agreement. She had talked a lot about love and not being able to live without him, and of how she lay awake at night thinking of him with Mel, his wife. Clark had her claws unsheathed, and Jack Carver wondered how deep she was prepared to sink them. This time he would have to make it quite clear that leaving Mel was not, as our American friends would say, an option.

The door of the pub opened. The hitcher entered. Jack Carver regretted that he had not travelled the previous evening. But the first session of the conference was not until Saturday afternoon. However, now he reckoned that better Friday traffic than Saturday morning trouble.

Alice Chambers was on her third visit to summon her neighbour in the flat just across the landing from her own. It was Saturday morning and Alice had a standing arrangement with Anne Tettle to go to the market. Concerned, though she wondered why she should be, Chambers returned to her own flat to get the spare key to Tettle's flat, part of a reciprocal arrangement which she had with her neighbour to cover any emergency which might arise.

'I can't get an answer from Anne,' she told Simon Burke, her lover, who was at the kitchen table nibbling on a piece of toast.

'Let her be,' was his advice. 'She'll not thank you.'

'She'll not thank me if we miss the market,' Alice said.

Alice Chambers opened the door of the flat and let herself in.

*

Conscious of the hitch-hiker's scrutiny, Jack Carver felt obliged to offer her an apology and a drink.

'A brandy to chase the chill away would be nice,' she said.

'Drenched her on the road,' Carver called out by way of explanation, as he became the focus of attention.

'Don't waste your breath.' She smiled mischievously. 'You should never explain. Always sounds like an excuse. They think you're picking me up.' She held out her hand. 'Brenda Collins.'

'Robert Blake,' Carver lied, telling himself that he was not sure why he had lied, but only fooling himself.

'So, is that what you're doing then – picking me up?' Carver was taken aback by her directness. 'Sorry. I'm being an absolute shit.'

'Another?' he felt obliged to ask.

'Wouldn't mind. Where are you headed?'

'Not far. Brigham. Business.'

'Let me guess.' Her intelligent grey eyes ran a quick appraisal over Carver. 'Sales?'

'Close enough. Mortgages.'

'I'm impressed.'

The compliment, though carefully crafted to flatter with a lift in mind, still made Carver feel chuffed.

'How far are you going?' he enquired.

'How far do you want me to go?' She enjoyed Carver's gob-smacked reaction. 'I'm being a shit, again. Sorry. As far as I can.' The grey eyes held Carver's. 'Are you offering, Robert?'

She said his fictitious name with a soft seduction.

'Yes.' Had he taken leave of his senses? She'd probably be nothing but trouble. 'If Brigham is of any use to you, that is?' No. He was not going to get involved. 'Look, on second thoughts—'

'It's OK. Someone always comes along.'

Why hadn't she got stroppy? It would have made it so much easier for him to leave.

'Excuse me. I couldn't help overhearing.'

Brenda Collins looked at the man who had been reading the tabloid newspaper with interest; the kind of interest she had shown Jack Carver only moments before. 'I could give you a lift.'

Carver thought: Cheeky sod. 'It's OK, mate. I've changed my mind.'

'Why don't we let the lady decide?'

Brenda Collins enjoyed her moment in the spotlight, letting her gaze drift between them, teasing each in turn. 'Thanks, Robert.'

The man's eyes bored into Carver, seething with the bitterness of rejection and wounded pride. Jack Carver left the pub with the cockiness of the only bull in a field full of panting cows.

'I reckon he thinks you're the devil incarnate.' Carver looked back. The old duffer was watching from the pub window, his look one of righteous disapproval. 'Sin and retribution type, I'd say. Probably have me burned at the stake as a harlot.'

Anxious to be away, Carver's hand slipped on the hand-brake, grazing his knuckles. As he pulled his hand away it brushed against Brenda Collins's leg, streaking her jeans with his blood. 'Sorry.' He slammed the car into gear and sped away, narrowly avoiding a collison with a brewery delivery truck turning into the pub.

'Better if it's done alive,' Collins said, cheekily.

There was absolutely no need to ask her what she thought was better done alive. The die had been cast. Discounting the old acne scar tissue on her chin, she was not bad-looking. He'd had worse. A short distance on, there was Cobley Wood. He'd pull in there.

'Anne,' Alice Chambers called from the open door of the flat. 'The best bargains will be gone at the market.'

Alice Chambers peered into the gloom, the weak grey light of day being unable to pierce the heavy drapes. There was some kind of smell in the flat that caught in her throat.

'Anne,' she called again, closing the door of the flat, feeling her way forward. 'Switch on the light, idiot,' she groaned, when her shin banged against the leg of an armchair.

She switched on the light, and immediately wished that she had not. Now she knew what the cloying smell was.

Congealed blood.

'You're an eager bunny, aren't you,' Brenda Collins said, her tone mildly mocking. She pushed Carver away. 'Nothing's for free, Robert.' Carver was taken aback. 'Shit, you didn't think I found you irresitible, did you?'

Jack Carver almost kicked her out of the car. Almost. But his blood was up. 'How much?'

'Depends.'

'On what?'

'On what your wife won't let you do. I'm feeling generous, Robert.' Her hand slid along his thigh, stopping teasingly short. 'Fifty quid, straight. Anything else is up for negotiation.'

'I don't have fifty quid.'

'Pull the other one, darling,' she scoffed, and added cheekily, 'But not before you pay.'

'Fifty quid it is, then.' Carver handed over the money and pulled her towards him.

'Steady, tiger!' She slipped from his clutches with the expertise of long experience. He grabbed her again. She yanked his head back by the hair. 'Must pee first.' She wiped her hands on a tissue to remove the hairs from Carver's head and tossed it out of the window.

'Oh, no you don't.' Carver pulled her back into the car. 'I didn't come down in the last shower. You'll do a runner with my fifty quid.'

'Without that?' Collins's eyes flashed to the rucksack on the back seat of the Vectra.

'The lot isn't worth a fiver,' Carver snorted. 'Leave the fifty quid on the dash until you come back.'

'No problem.'

Carver was surprised by her ready acceptance of his ultimatum. 'I'm pushed for time,' he reminded her. Ten minutes later, frustrated, Carver went to the edge of the trees and called out. He got no reply. He went a short distance further, cursing as he sank in the soft mud. He called out again, but got no response. His humour was soured further when the branch of a water-laden tree dumped chilling water down his neck. 'An elephant wouldn't have a bladder that size,' he grumbled. Angry, he hurried back to the Vectra and tossed the rucksack in a pool of muddy water. He was getting back into the car when he spotted banknotes poking out of a small pocket of the rucksack where the zip had broken. He checked. 'Three hundred. Busy girl.' He pocketed two fifties. 'Call it compensation for my frustration, darling,' he said sourly. Carver got in the driving seat and drove off. As he checked the rearview mirror before he came out of the wood he saw a white Almera parked under heavily laden trees whose branches looped down over the car. The same Almera that had almost collided with him when he had turned into the pub? He hadn't noticed the car when he had driven into the wood. Of course that was not surprising, preoccupied as he was.

Brenda Collins came from the trees and, seeing her discarded rucksack, she immediately checked the contents of the small pocket. As he sped away, her furious reaction pleased Jack Carver.

About a mile on he came to a service station and pulled in, feeling chuffed that Brenda Collins's money would be filling the Vectra's tank.

'Sorry, mate,' a man coming from the forecourt shop apologized. 'Lightning. Pumps are on the blink.'

'Not my day,' Carver growled. 'I'll use the loo, if it's not bunged up, that is.'

'Round the side.'

Carver reversed the Vectra back from the pumps in line with the loo. As he got back into the car, he noticed rain-spatters on the driver's seat, and wondered briefly where the spatters had come from. The window was closed.

'Police. Can I help you?'
    'There's been a murder,' said Alice Chambers.

CHAPTER TWO

'The traditional blunt instrument, Inspector.' Alec Balson, the police surgeon, straightened up from his examination of the woman's body, grimacing as his fifty-seven-year-old back protested. 'I'm getting too bloody old for this,' he groused, in a gruff rumbling voice.

Half an hour earlier, DI Sally Speckle's stomach had churned on seeing the woman's bludgeoned head, the skull with several punctures in it. Her stomach had not yet settled.

'Do we have a name for her?' Balson enquired.

'Anne Tettle. Weapon?' Speckle enquired.

'The fractures in the skull would be consistent with blows from a hammer.' He shook his head. 'Several blows, when one would have done.'

'A killer in a rage?'

'I'm not sure,' said the police surgeon ponderously. 'The blows were delivered left-handedly. . . .'

'And?' Speckle prompted.

Balson frowned. 'The blows were weakish. Maybe the

number of blows might have been to ensure certainty, rather than being struck in rage. It might be that the murderer is naturally right-handed. Imagine if the killer grabbed the murder weapon with his left hand. I'm a right-hander. So. . . .' Alec Balson struck out, holding the imaginary weapon in his left hand. His blows were awkward and erratic. Then, repeating the exercise with his right hand, his imaginary blows were accurate and forceful. 'See what I mean?'

Speckle and Lukeson certainly did.

'So we could be looking for a right-handed murderer, who is trying to fool us into thinking that we're looking for a left-handed killer?' Lukeson asked.

'Possibly,' Balson said. 'Of course it might simply be that the murderer grabbed the murder weapon with his left hand and dared not risk pausing to switch it to his right hand, fearful that the victim might, given the opportunity, put up a struggle.

'After the first stunning blow, it would have been a token fight back. However, clawing and scratching might occur. And the killer would not have wanted that to happen. All that lovely DNA.'

'Any sign of sexual activity?' Speckle enquired.

'Nothing obvious.'

'Might she have been murdered by a woman? Could that account for the weaker blows?'

Balson considered Andy Lukeson's question.

'I suppose it might be something worth thinking about,' he conceded cautiously. 'But if it was a woman, based on the victim's height and the angle of the blows, her assailant would have to be taller than the average female. But then, if the victim had been in a crouch,' Balson cowered, arms raised as if to ward off blows, 'like so, that would make a difference. Frankly, your guess is as good as mine, Sergeant.'

'Why a woman, Andy?' Speckle asked.

'Photographs.' Lukeson pointed to photographs dotted round the flat, drawing particular attention to two showing the victim in what Lukeson would describe as a clinch with another woman. 'Not a man in sight.'

'Lesbian?'

'Just a thought,' Lukeson said.

'TOD?' Speckle enquired of the PS.

Alec Balson drew in a deep breath and chewed on his lower lip. 'You could be thinking about somewhere around fourteen to . . . oh, sixteen hours,' he opined.

'Nine a.m. now. So she was murdered between five and seven o'clock last evening?'

'Give or take,' Balson agreed.

'No sign of forced entry. Coded access to the house. Knew her killer?' the DI speculated.

'Or an in-house killer, perhaps?' Balson said.

'Has the interviewing of the other residents begun, Andy?'

'As we speak.'

'Poor bitch.' Alec Balson's pity was fleeting. Balson was not an unsympathetic or uncaring man, but had he allowed himself to be affected by the numerous murders he had attended, he would soon have ended up in an asylum. He checked his watch. 'Phone, anyone? Mine needs charging.'

Andy Lukeson proffered his mobile. Balson punched out a number, waited a moment, and then explained, 'Sorry, m'dear. I'm afraid you'll have to start without me.' Seeing the amused response his conversation got from the SOCOs, he put his hand over the phone and growled, 'Shopping.' Then into the phone again, 'Be along as soon as I can, m'dear.'

He handed Lukeson back his phone.

'Prelim report as soon as possible, Inspector. I doubt if the post mortem will hold any surprises. It's a straight smash and bash.'

'Found this on the bedside locker.' Lukeson handed Speckle a piece of paper with a telephone number scribbled on it. 'Getting no reply. Waiting for a call back from the phone company with a name and address.'

He had no sooner spoken than his mobile rang.

'The number belongs to a Jennifer Roberts, number twelve Allworth Avenue,' he informed DI Sally Speckle.

CHAPTER THREE

As Jack Carver turned into the hotel car park, a woman in a yellow jacket darted across in front of him. Anxiety gripped Carver. The woman was about the same height and build as Collins. 'Can't be her,' he murmured. Must be hundreds of women wearing yellow jackets,' he added, a hint of doubt creeping into his voice. 'All I bloody need now is for Brenda Collins to turn up!'

Jack Carver anxiously reran his conversation with Collins. He had told her he was coming to Brigham. And that he was in mortgages. A quick check round the hotels. Mortages. Building Society bash. Not rocket science.

The two fifty-pound notes he had stolen from Brenda Collins burned a hole in his pocket. He had acted on a stupid impulse; an impulse he hoped was not going to cost him dear.

The receptionist's fingers flashed across a computer keyboard. 'Welcome to the Silver Towers, Mr Carver. You're in three twelve, sir. And if I might have your car details, sir. Security is everything these days. More and more of it all the time.'

Jack Carver reeled off the car's registration, and added, 'Maroon Vectra.'

'Well, if it isn't horny Jack Carver,' a husky female voice whispered in his ear – the unmistakable voice of Mattie Clark.

Carver swung round and swallowed hard. He would not have thought it possible that Mattie Clark could be even more stunning than she had been at their last meeting, but more stunning she certainly was. Carver wondered if he could delay telling her that it was over between them until after he had made love to her one last time, his resolve to clear the decks swiftly melting away.

'Hello, Mattie. How're tricks?'

'Remains to be seen, Jack.' She chuckled throatily. 'I've missed you. We have lots to talk about.' Carver was unsure as to how to react. She came closer. Mattie Clark's body scent washed over him. She wore an expensive perfume, but it was no match for her heady hormonal musk. The slightest brush against him had the effect of dropping a spanner on an electricity high-tension cable.

'Matilda Clark,' she announced to the waiting receptionist. 'Same outfit.' Carver had read the flouncing male receptionist wrong. The shake in his hand when he checked the computer for her reservation was one hundred per cent red-blooded male. 'See you shortly. Like I said, lots to talk about.'

As she walked away to the lifts, all male eyes were on her.

On the periphery of his vision, Jack Carver glimpsed a flash of yellow. He swung round but the woman wearing the yellow jacket had gone past. Julius Roycroft, the new CEO, was coming from the lift that Mattie Clark had summoned. Panic kicked in. He had to stop Collins. He hurried across the foyer, grabbed her by the arm and commanded:

'Outside. Now.'

'Take your hands off me!'

The woman rounding on him was most definitely not Brenda Collins. He looked aghast at the package the woman was carrying, and the name of the courier company emblazoned on her jacket. 'S-s-sorry,' he stammered, wanting to put his hand over the woman's mouth to muffle her strident outcry. 'I thought you were someone else.'

'Well, I'm bloody not!' she ranted, her outraged voice going up several decibels.

The hotel foyer had become hushed. Carver could feel Roycroft's eyes on him. Hotel security, in the shape of a hard-faced man whose features had taken too many punches, appeared out of nowhere, like the villian in a panto out of smoke.

'What seems to be the problem?'

His mean-eyed glare at Jack Carver showed that he had decided that he was.

'Whatever it is, it's his,' the courier said angrily.

'Perhaps if you'd move aside, sir,' the security man requested of Carver, taking up a position between him and the courier.

'It was a silly mistake,' Jack Carver said, limply.

'Of course, sir,' the security man said, obviously not believing a word of it.

Glaring back at Carver every few paces, the courier continued on to reception. Mattie Clark was staring at Carver, curiously. Julius Roycroft was staring at him also, but his expression was one of total annoyance.

'Bloody marvellous!' Jack Carver mumured.

'What was that all about?' Mattie Clark asked when he joined her in the lift. 'A woman scorned? A mighty dangerous example of the species,' she added pointedly.

'A mistake. I thought she was someone else.'

'You were ready to wring her neck. But I'm not complaining, I like you all fired up.' She forced him back against the wall of the lift.

Carver slipped away. 'Not now, Mattie. Later.'

'I'm beginning to feel like an old shoe, lover. And I don't like the feeling.' She strode out of the lift the second the doors opened, but paused a couple of paces on. 'It's not wise to upset me, Jack.'

CHAPTER FOUR

'Miss Jennifer Roberts?' DS Andy Lukeson enquired of the woman who had opened the door of number twelve Allworth Avenue.

'Lord. It's been an age since anyone called me Jennifer. My sister Sara used to, rest her soul. She hated names being abbreviated.' Her gaze went from Lukeson to DC Helen Rochester and back again. 'Police?'

Lukeson smiled and looked down at his feet.

'Is it that obvious. I'm DS Andy Lukeson, and my colleague is Detective Constable Helen Rochester. May we come inside?'

Jen Roberts led the way into the sitting-room and indicated that they should sit in two comfortable armchairs. She remained standing. Helen Rochester shifted on the seat. 'Sorry.' Jen Roberts picked up the novel and rolled-up crêpe bandage upon which Rochester had sat and put them in the drawer of the coffee table. 'What's all this about,' she enquired of Lukeson.

'Do you know an Anne Tettle?' Lukeson enquired.

'Yes.'

'A friend?'

'More an acquaintance, Sergeant.' She became concerned. 'Has something happened Anne?'

'Why would you think that, Ms Roberts?'

'The police don't call round for a social chat, do they?'

'I'm sorry to say that Ms Tettle has been found dead at her flat.'

'Dead!'

'Murdered.'

Roberts collapsed on to a sofa. 'But who'd want to murder Anne?'

'That's what we're attempting to find out. Can DC Rochester get you something? A cup of tea? Something stronger, perhaps?'

'Nothing, thanks.' Curiosity overcame shock. 'How did you find me, Sergeant?'

'Your phone number was on Ms Tettle's bedside locker. We phoned several times, but there was no reply.'

'I was out. I've just come in.'

'We should all get more exercise.'

'Oh, only to the next street. I hate exercise.'

'Hope you don't mind. Under the circumstances we needed to make contact quickly. We got your address from the telephone company.'

'No. Not at all. I jotted down my number for Anne last evening, Sergeant. Because I thought she might need it.'

'You visited Ms Tettle last evening, then?'

'No. I met her at the hospice. She works . . . used to work there.'

'Why did you think she might need your number?'

'To talk. I got the impression that Anne was worried about something.'

'Such as?'

'She never phoned, so I don't know.'

'Do you work at the hospice, too?' DC Helen Rochester enquired.

'No. Mrs Gerrard, the hospice owner and matron, started what she called her adopt a patient scheme about a year ago. I volunteered. I quit when the patient I adopted died. Lung cancer. Blamed his time in the Saudi oil industry for it.'

She smiled reflectively.

'Arthur had a sixty a day habit all his adult life. But he'd never concede that it was smoking and not oil that gave him his cancer. Now Mrs Gerrard wants me to reconsider and adopt another patient. That's why I was at the hospice last evening.

'Many of the patients at the hospice have no one to visit them. You'd be surprised how cruelly relatives dump and abandon their kinfolk. Frankly, I'm not too keen on the idea. You see, I became very fond of Arthur Granger. He might have been my own father. His death took a great deal out of me.'

Andy Lukeson made sympathetic noises.

'Ms Tettle was a nurse at the hospice?'

'Oh, no. Reception. Admin. That kind of thing. A bit of a dogsbody, really.' She laughed. 'Anne used to say that Letitia Gerrard invented multi-skilling.' Her laughter deepened. 'She nicknamed her Gerrard the Hun.

'Anyway, Mrs Gerrard can be quite persistent and insis-tent. So I went along to the hospice last evening to talk to her. While I was there I met Anne. She seemed' – she considered her description of Anne Tettle's mood and came up with – 'rattled.'

Lukeson latched on to the word. 'Rattled?'

'On edge. Jumpy.'

'Any ideas about what might have been causing her concern?'

'Not really. Well, I thought it might be . . .' Jen Roberts dismissed her thought. 'But that couldn't be right.'

'What couldn't be right?' DC Rochester asked.

'Man trouble, Constable. Anne Tettle was gay.'

Andy Lukeson recalled the photographs in Tettle's flat and gave himself a little clap on the back. 'So, knowing this, what made you think Ms Tettle was having man trouble?'

Jen Roberts looked steadily at Lukeson. 'Anne was on the phone when I arrived at the hospice. Just as I got near she said, leave me alone you bastard, or I'll go to the police.'

'Sounds serious.'

'I thought she might be in real trouble, hence my tele-phone number.'

'And you have no idea who this man might be?'

'None, Sergeant.'

'Pity.'

'Yes. It is.'

'Did you visit Miss Tettle at her flat?' Helen Rochester enquired.

'Not regularly. A time or two. Anne and I really didn't

have much in common to form the basis for a friendship.'

'When did you last visit?'

'Oh . . .' Roberts screwed up her eyes. 'A couple of weeks ago. And that was only to deliver a book she'd lent me. I didn't stay.'

'Did Ms Tettle ever come here?'

'No.'

'Do you know anything about her private life?' Lukeson enquired. 'Things like places she frequented. People she might have met? That kind of thing.'

'Like I said, I really didn't know her that well.'

'But well enough to think that she might want to share her secrets with you,' Rochester observed, pointedly.

'Secrets?' Roberts scoffed. 'That sounds very Famous Fivish, don't you think.'

'Ever meet anyone else at the flat?'

'Once. A man. Simon Burke, he's a . . . *friend* of Alice Chambers. She lives in the flat across from Anne's.'

'Yes. It was she who actually found Ms Tettle's body.'

'Good grief. Poor bitch.'

'May I ask what your perception of Mr Burke's visit was?'

'My perception? I'm not sure I understand your question, Sergeant. I really didn't think about it.'

'But with hindsight,' Lukeson pressed.

'You're asking me to speculate, Sergeant,' she responded brusquely. 'Look, Anne was gay. Very much so. Besides, Simon Burke is Alice Chambers' lover. And Anne and Alice were friends.'

'Some of the most passionate affairs involve friends, Ms

Roberts,' Lukeson said.

'Frankly, I was too surprised to find Anne entertaining a man in the first place.'

'Entertaining?' Rochester pounced.

'Just an off the cuff word, Constable,' said Roberts frostily. 'Anyway, it would be a foolish dog who'd soil his own doorstep, don't you think? And Anne's opinion of Burke was not high.'

'She told you this?'

'Yes. I honestly think that even if Anne were straight, she'd have had nothing to do with Simon Burke.'

'Thank you for your help.' Lukeson stood up to leave. 'If you think of anything else—'

'Of course, Sergeant.' Jen Roberts shook her head. 'You know, I really can't imagine Anne upsetting anyone enough for them to want to murder her.'

'You might drop by the station to give a statement when you get an opportunity.'

'Of course. Not that there's much to tell, is there?'

'Of like persuasion to Tettle, you think, Sarge?' Helen Rochester speculated, once outside. 'Living alone. Late thirties.'

'Many women are living alone and in their late thirties.'

'Prudish. It's a doll's house, isn't it. You couldn't see a man about the place could you, Sarge. Jocks hanging on the bedpost. Dirty socks under the pillow. Beer cans on that immaculately polished coffee table. And, of course, I hate her. All legs and Twiggy thin.' DC Helen Rochester groaned, struggling as she was, yet again, with another sure-fire diet. 'Why would she need to jog?'

'Jog? She just said that she hates exercise.'

'Well, there's a brand-new tracksuit in a Labatt's shopping bag in the corner near the sitting-room fireplace. Shit,' she exclaimed as she squeezed between a red Fiesta parked on the drive and a low-hanging tree which dumped rainwater on her. 'Where's the logic of leaving the car in the drive rotting away, when you have a garage to put it in.'

Andy Lukeson chuckled. 'Logic and females are not compatible.'

'Oh, piss off, Sarge!'

Driving away, Lukeson asked, 'What do you make of this man Burke?'

'I think Roberts had a point when she doubted if he'd start something with his lover's friend, living just across the landing. But then men aren't the brightest, are they, Sarge? We all know where their brains are.'

'That could be considered abuse of a superior,' Lukeson said, tongue in cheek. Then thoughtfully: 'Wonder if Burke was around when Tettle was murdered?'

All legs and Twiggy thin, Helen Rochester's description of Roberts. He wondered if such an obviously intelligent woman as Jen Roberts was, would, had she murdered Anne Tettle, have left her telephone number hanging about? What effect would murder have on the intellect? Particularly if it was the kind of murder that would spring from a sudden and unexpected confrontation. Such an event could, Andy Lukeson reckoned, scatter a body's wits.

CHAPTER FIVE

Having just settled down to watch *Brief Encounter* (her all-time favourite) on the telly, the buzz of the doorbell annoyed Mel Carver. She peered out through the side of the sitting-room window and saw Jen Roberts, her next-door neighbour, huddled against the driving rain which was in its third dreary day with only brief respites, making it miserable and gloomy. Meanly, she wondered if she could get away with pretending not to be at home?

'Jen,' Mel enthused a moment later on opening the front door. 'How nice.'

Hypocrite!

'Something terrible's happened, Mel,' Roberts said, hurrying past. 'The most awful thing. I've just had the police round. Anne Tettle has been murdered.'

'Anne Tettle? Wasn't she the woman you had Jack repair some doors for? Murdered, did you say?'

Jen Roberts shivered and hugged herself. 'Who could have done such an awful thing, Mel?'

'You go and sit down. I'll make a cuppa. Or perhaps

you'd prefer a drink?'

'No, tea will be fine. You watch the telly. I'll brew up. It'll give me something to do.' She glanced in at the sitting-room door. 'Isn't that *Brief Encounter*? She pushed Mel Carver into the sitting-room. 'You go and get all weepy.'

Roberts delayed a moment.

'You know, Jack is not unlike Trevor Howard, is he? Could that be why you married him?'

Mel laughed. 'Jack's not all that like Trevor Howard. Jack's face is fuller, for one thing.'

'Not my cup of tea,' Jen said, heading for the kitchen.

'I fancy the film, not Trevor Howard,' Mel called after her. 'I suppose you're a Brad Pitt or Tom Cruise fan?'

Jen Roberts turned and shook her head.

'Russell Crowe?'

Jen Roberts shook her head again.

'Who, then?'

'The weather forecaster on the Beeb. The dark one with the brooding looks.' Jen Roberts sighed dreamily. 'No one can say *low front approaching* like he can.'

'Oh, get off! You'll find a packet of chocolate-chip biscuits in the press to the right of the sink.'

'Feel like going down the pub later?'

'Don't know if I'm in the humour, Jen. It's all this gloomy weather. And won't your friend's murder put a damper on things?'

'Getting out will do us both good. Jack in his room hiding, while you get all soppy?'

'Jack's in Brigham.'

'What's he doing in Brigham?'

'A company conference. I told you, remember?'

Jen Roberts shook her head. 'I don't think you did, Mel.'

'I'm sure I—'

'Oh.' Jen Roberts took a car key from the pocket of her jeans and handed it to Mel.

'For heaven's sake. I've been looking high and low. It's Janet's spare key. My ditzy sister left it behind when she was here last week. Then I lost it. Last I saw, it was on the kitchen table. Where did you find it?'

'Stood on it on the way in. Back in a mo with piping-hot tea.'

'So, did Mrs Gerrard talk you in to rejoining her adopt a patient scheme?' Mel enquired.

'Well, I went to the hospice last evening to tell Gerrard that I had definitely decided to quit, and ended up staying for over an hour with a patient. Poor thing is very poorly. Sleeps most of the time. Not long more to go.'

'I wouldn't have the bottle, Jen.'

'It can be pretty depressing, but it also has its compensations. Arthur Granger was a darling.'

'You grew quite fond of him, didn't you?'

'You could say that Arthur changed the entire course of my life, Mel,' she said, reflectively. 'Look, I'll leave you in peace to watch the telly.'

'Oh, I've seen *Brief Encounter* a thousand times before, Jen.'

Mel felt obliged to encourage Jen Roberts to stay, but selfishly hoped she would not.

'No. I've got a hundred and one things to do, Mel.' She sprang out of the armchair she was sitting in. 'But thanks.

Think about going down the pub.'

Sitting close to the sitting-room window, Mel watched Jen Roberts leave. Hunched against the rain, she looked deformed and reminded Mel of a man with a stoop who had lived near her as a child, and had given her the creepiest feeling whenever she saw him.

Mel Carver was gripped by the oddest, inexplicable little shiver.

'Do nicely.'

DI Sally Speckle went and looked at the drinking glass the fingerprint officer had dusted, showing three clear prints on the glass.

'If they're the killer's. Without a match on the database it will all be useless unless we catch him.'

Sally Speckle felt somewhat overwhelmed. In charge of her first murder investigation, she was labouring under two distinct disadvantages – lack of experience, and the kind of respect officers who had learned their trade the traditional way got.

She was what the tough-as-nuts officers disparagingly called a *graddie*. Meaning she had entered the force through the graduate recruitment programme, beloved by senior officers and Whitehall mandarins but despised by most officers who saw graduate entrants as earmarked for quick promotion without having been put through the wringer. And there was a suspicion that graddies were definitely pro-management.

'I'm sure you'll experience no difficulties, Sally,' the Assistant Chief Constable had said, brushing aside her doubts about fast-tracking her to promotion and how it might be resented by officers who had taken the traditional route and who would feel that the DI's vacancy should be filled by one of them. 'I'll assign you a sergeant who knows the ropes. A chap like Andy Lukeson.'

She had heard of Lukeson's reputation as one of Loston CID's most astute and fair-minded officers, so it had gone some way to reassure her.

'I have every confidence in you, Sally,' the ACC had said. 'I want you to grasp this opportunity and put paid to this idea that graduate officers are not every inch as much coppers as those who lay claim to exclusivity in that area.

'And we don't want those lefties in the House to be proved right, do we?'

The ACC had been referring to a recent debate in the House of Commons, during which a left-wing MP had described graduate officers as the *fodder that got senior officers a gong and genuine coppers a smaller pension.*

Thankfully, DS Andy Lukeson was an honest copper in every sense of the word, and had not sought opportunities, as others had when assigned to graddies, to drop her in it.

'Police work is a team effort,' Lukeson had told her during their first case together, a GBH. 'You come up with an idea. I get a hunch. Someone else looks at the problem from another angle. Bits and pieces that finally come together.'

He had smiled.

'A lot of the time by pure mistake or a lucky break and not by Holmesian brilliance. The woman has recently visited Sussex, Watson,' he had intoned haughtily.

'By Gad! How can you possibly know that, Holmes?'

'Her shoes are covered with a white dust, peculiar to Sussex, my dear fellow. And she has visited a farm.'

Andy Lukeson, in the persona of Watson, looked suitably bemused.

'There was a feather attached to the back of her cloak; a feather which is peculiar to Sussex hens, my dear, Watson.'

'Brilliant, Holmes!'

Andy Lukeson had waved his hands airily. 'Elementary, dear Watson. Elementary.'

Sally Speckle recalled with pleasure the madcap moment after making an arrest in the GBH, and it raised her spirits now.

'What's there to smile about, then?'

Speckle swung around on hearing Lukeson. 'Just something that came to mind. How did the Roberts interview go?'

'Interesting could describe it.' Lukeson gave Speckle the gist of the interview, ending: 'And Tettle was gay.'

'Who's a clever boy, then,' the DI teased her sergeant. 'Any thoughts on Burke?'

'Roberts seems certain that it was a non-starter.'

'Burke might not have seen it that way?'

'But why try and start something that could not succeed? Being Chambers' lover, he must have known that Tettle was gay.'

'Maybe Burke saw Anne Tettle as a challenge to put right. You know the kind of thing. Once she knew what it was all about, she'd wonder why she had ever been gay.'

Lukeson was not convinced.

'Anything come of the in-house door to door?' he enquired.

Speckle sighed. 'It seems everyone is deaf, dumb and blind.'

'What's new,' Lukeson sympathized. 'People blame the police when crime goes unsolved. But when they're asked to help, they don't want to know. And Chambers?'

'I left her for the time being. I'll check with WPC Fenning to see if she's up to being interviewed now.' Speckle went across the landing to Chambers' flat, and a moment later beckoned to Lukeson to follow.

'This won't take long, will it?' Alice Chambers fretted.

'We'll be as brief as we can be,' Speckle said, and enquired, 'Why did you enter Ms Tettle's flat this morning?'

'To wake her up, when she didn't answer. It's Saturday. We always go to the market on Grey's Quay on Saturday. I couldn't get an answer, so I used the key to the flat to get in. We exchanged keys in case of an emergency.'

'You and Ms Tettle were close friends?' Lukeson asked.

'Anne liked her own company best, Sergeant.'

'Sounds like a difficult person to befriend. How long have you been acquainted?'

'Most of the time she's been here. We met at work, actually.'

'You also work at Loston Hospice, then?' Speckle enquired.

'Oh, no. No. I meant that we met at Labett's, where I work. Anne brought a pair of jeans back, incorrectly labelled. The wrong leg size. The assistant who was dealing with her was rather curt, thankfully we've got rid of her since. As a supervisor, I was called on to step in to sort matters out. 'Anne was very gracious. That evening, returning from work, I met her on the stairs. I hadn't known she was living here, nor she I. She'd only been here about a week. I asked her if she'd like to go for a drink later. She accepted. The following Saturday we went to the market together, and it became something of a ritual. Quite tiresome sometimes, to be quite honest.'

'If you found it tiresome, why did you keep going?' Speckle asked.

'Well, Anne was not an easy person to say no to, Inspector. She'd say that's OK, in her quite disappointed way. I'd feel guilty and end up going anyway. But she could be good fun, too,' Alice Chambers added hastily. 'Not in a million years could I imagine that she'd upset anyone enough to want to murder her.'

'That seems to be the general opinion,' Lukeson said. 'You were alone when you found the body?'

'Yes.'

'That must have been a terrible shock.'

'It was.'

'You live alone?'

'Yes.'

'Prefer it that way, do you?'

'I suppose,' Chambers said, as if she had never considered what it might be like to share.

'It's come to our attention that you have a certain male friend,' Speckle said.

'I see,' Chambers reacted, annoyed. 'What little busybody told you that, Inspector?'

'Was this man here last evening?'

'Yes.'

'At what time did he arrive?'

'I can't be sure. I wasn't here when he arrived.'

'Doesn't matter. We can check with him.'

Panic streaked across Alice Chambers eyes. 'I can't give you his address, Inspector.'

'Can't? This is a murder inquiry,' the DI said sternly.

'You can't think that Simon was in any way involved?'

'We're not saying he was,' Lukeson said.

'Then why bother him? You don't understand.'

'We're certainly trying.'

'Oh, God,' Chambers groaned. 'This is terrible.' She visually pleaded with both Speckle and Lukeson, both of whom remained implacable.

'We'll be as discreet as circumstances will permit,' was Speckle's only concession.

Defeated, Alice Chambers murmured, 'Horton Way. The name of the house is Bettyville. The Betty in ville, is my sister. Simon's my brother-in-law.'

Recalling Alice Chambers bolder than bold eye contact as she had confirmed that she had been alone when she had found Anne Tettle's body, Lukeson played a hunch. 'Was Mr Burke with you when you found the body?' he enquired.

'Well . . .'

Alice Chambers' eye contact was no longer bold, but slid away from Lukeson's gaze. It was as he had thought. Her earlier confirmation that she had been alone when she had discovered Tettle's body had been a defiant gesture to cover a lie.

'Look, Simon was here,' she admitted, shakily.

'He wasn't here when the uniformed officers arrived,' Lukeson said.

'He. . . . We thought it best if he wasn't,' Chambers said. Her eyes flashed between Speckle and Lukeson. 'I'm sure you'll understand why. And, of course, there was Simon's future to consider, too.'

'His future?' Speckle questioned.

'There's a chance Simon will be selected as a candidate for the next general election. Were he to be involved in a scandal.' Alice Chambers gave a hopeless little shrug. 'Well, that would be that, wouldn't it.'

'Did Mr Burke know Ms Tettle well?' Speckle enquired.

'Hardly at all.'

'We have a witness who says that Mr Burke visited Ms Tettle.'

'A witness?' Chambers was suddenly alarmed.

'What time did you get home last evening?' the DI queried.

'About 7.30.'

'Was Mr Burke here when you arrived home?'

'No. Simon had popped out to the chemist to get paracetamol for a nagging tooth.'

'Which chemist would that be?'

'He didn't say.'

'Did you see the paracetamol?'

'No.'

'Was Mr Burke expecting you to be late home?' the DI enquired.

'Yes. I phoned to say I'd be late.'

'Did Mr Burke know that Anne Tettle was gay?'

'I never said, Inspector.'

'But he could have known?'

Alice Chambers shrugged. 'What has Anne being gay got to do with all of this?'

'How long have you and Mr Burke been . . . *friends*?'

'Two years.'

'WPC Fenning will take your statement now, Ms Chambers.'

'Inspector. You can't possibly think that Simon was in any way involved in Anne's death, surely?'

Lukeson was at the door when he asked, 'Did Mr Burke know you had a key to Ms Tettle's flat?'

'I'm not sure. He might have, I suppose.'

On leaving Chambers' flat, Speckle said, 'Are you thinking what I'm thinking, Andy?'

'That Burke, knowing that he had time on his hands, popped across the landing for a bit extra? Maybe even used the spare key to surprise Tettle? And it all went wrong. But even if Burke did try it on with Tettle, murder is a long way from a bit of hanky-panky.'

'Oh, I don't know, Andy. Rejection and anger go hand in hand. And maybe it was not something that happened last evening. What if it was something that had happened previously? Maybe Tettle threatened to tell Chambers? Worse still, to go to the police?

'Roberts told us that Tettle had had angry exchanges on the phone with some man. A short time later, Tettle is murdered. Simon Burke was here in the house, alone. As Chambers pointed out, Simon Burke had a lot to lose. A lover. His marriage. An opportunity to be an MP. And who knows, maybe a seat at the cabinet table later on. And possibly time in prison. Over all, that's quite a motive for murder. Maybe he went to plead with Tettle and she wasn't having any of it?'

'But if Burke did murder Tettle, would he hang around to wait for Chambers to find her body?' the Dl wondered.

'The plan had obviously been to spend the night with Chambers. If Burke had changed his plans it would have brought attention to him,' Andy Lukeson reasoned. 'And that's the last thing he would have wanted.

'Maybe Burke popped out to buy a hammer instead of paracetamol?'

'Have the hardware stores checked, Andy.' Why couldn't her first murder have been simple, Sally Speckle thought dolefully. With the killer standing over the body holding a smoking gun, ready to confess. 'Or maybe Burke went to dump his bloodstained clothes? But to do that, he'd need a change of clothing.'

'Burke's got spare clothing in Chambers' flat,' Lukeson said. 'When we were interviewing Chambers, the bedroom door was open behind her. There was a man's clothing in the wardrobe.'

'Arrange for skips, alleyways, waste ground and derelict buildings to be searched,' Speckle said. 'Anywhere where something might have been dumped. He probably wouldn't have gone far. Check out the chemists, too. Even if Burke isn't remembered, all the chemists will have CCTV footage.'

'Burke could have been clever and have bought paracetamol to cover himself,' Lukeson said.

Speckle's mobile rang.

'Hello, Speckle. Yes, sir.' She mouthed silently. '*Doyle*. Yes, right away, sir.' She broke the connection. 'Bloody hell! A second murder.'

'Where?'

'Cobley Wood.'

'Isn't that on Brigham's patch?'

'Just our side of the line,' said Speckle wearily. 'A second murder on my plate is all I need.'

'*Our* plate, Sally,' Lukeson said.

CHAPTER SIX

The last place Jack Carver wanted to be was at dinner, even with Mattie Clark rubbing his thigh under the table. 'I must be losing my touch,' she murmured in a waspish aside at his lack of interest. 'Missing the little woman, are we?' And the last thing he needed or wanted was another complication, no matter how delectable. He had thought about crying off ill, but had decided that coming after the incident in the hotel foyer, he could have suffered ten different kinds of fit and no one would have believed him.

Roycroft's rallying the troops speech was blessedly short, but pointed. Lots of references about rash and impetuous actions that might compromise the society or besmirch its reputation. Carver did not need to look up from his consideration of the pattern on the linen table-cloth. There was no need to confirm at whom Roycroft was looking.

When Roycroft, crafty bastard that he was, took advantage of Mattie Clark's peevishness with Carver, she shot Carver a smug look. He might have been imagining it, but he also reckoned that Roycroft did the same – a kind of *here's up yours, old man* look. He reckoned that he knew now who would be getting any promotion going.

Roycroft led the way out of the dining-room like a master with his charges. In the bar, the news was on telly.

'The body of the young hitch-hiker was found in Cobley Wood between Loston and Brigham today.' Jack Carver stopped dead in his tracks. 'Police wish to interview a man, described as being in his early forties of pale complexion with dark hair going grey, and drives what is believed to be a dark-coloured, possibly maroon Vauxhall Vectra car. The man gave the woman a lift from the Coach and Four public house, only a short distance from where she was found.'

Jack Carver's blood ran cold.

'The police think that this man can help them with their inquiries, and asks that he get in contact with the Cobley Wood incident room or any police station.'

The words echoed inside Jack Carver's head like rolling thunder. *Help the police with their enquiries.* Copperspeak for when they had their mind made up. He was, by some nightmarish twist of fate, the chief suspect in a murder. The newscaster had not actually said murder, but there could be no doubting what he meant.

Casting his mind back to when he drove away, Jack Carver recalled seeing a parked car in Cobley Wood partly hidden under heavily rain-laden trees. A white Almera. Had the killer been in the car? Might he be the man whom Brenda Collins rejected at the pub? Or could it be the driver of the white Almera that had shot past as he turned into the pub car park? Or perhaps the righteous old duffer who had been watching from the pub window on a mission of punishing the fallen woman? On the face of it, that would seem unlikely. But he recalled the old geezer's look of virtuous indignation when he and Brenda Collins left the pub. It was difficult to imagine the old duffer as a murderer. However, Carver knew that sometimes the most unlikely people became murderers, if the motivation was strong enough. And there was nothing stronger than religious zeal. Millions through the ages had fallen foul of that. And why had Collins taken so long to arrive back? Could it be that she had met someone in the wood?

Her killer, perhaps?

Thankfully everyone was too busy sidling up to the bar for Roycroft's largess to be bothered with the news. He must contact the police. Carver was leaving the bar to do just that when the perilousness of his situation struck home. A white Almera. He did not have the car's registration number. How many white Almeras were there? An old duffer on a mission of punishing a scarlet woman? Fanciful. The man whom Collins had rejected was a plausible suspect. But overall he could see how sceptical a hardnosed copper would be, having sat through a thousand tall yarns. The police were looking for him. And they might just settle for that.

A nightmarish catalogue flashed through Jack Carver's mind. Blood from his grazed hand on Brenda Collins's jeans. The tissue she had wiped her hands on and had then tossed out of the car window had hairs from his head on it. He had grabbed hold of Brenda Collins. Fibres from his clothing would be on hers. He could hear the squelching sound of his footprint in the muddy soil at the edge of the wood when he had gone to call her. He had handled her rucksack, particularly the plastic-coated flap of the pocket from which he had stolen. Fingerprints. There would be trace evidence in and on the Vectra. Minute particles that the human eye could not see, but which would not be missed by the hi-tech forensics team. Soil. Leaves. Fragments of bark. Twigs. Mud peculiar to Cobley Wood. Tyre-tread patterns. From the pattern they would find the manufacturer. Then the company sales records. Then to what outlet they had been distributed. And, eventually, the car they had been fitted to. There was a little hope. Might the evidence have been washed away? Obliterated by the downpour? But the rain had ceased for a period after he had driven away. How long had it been before the police had arrived at the scene of the murder?

'Members of the jury. You have sat through a litany of damning evidence. Can there be any doubt in your minds that the accused brutally attacked and murdered an innocent woman? A complete stranger; a woman he picked up with only one purpose in mind; a plan that went drastically awry and ended in the woman's brutal demise.'

A prosecuting QC, greener than a leprechaun's jacket, would have no difficulty convincing a jury. Go to the police? He would not stand a chance of being believed. And why should the police look any further than a suspect with so much evidence stacked against the one they would have in custody. And if he did not present himself to help with their enquiries, the natural assumption would be that he had not come forward because he was guilty.

He could not win.

'If you're not careful you'll drink that beer, Jack.'

Thankfully, the gossipy Larry Slater breezed past, eager to join a group sucking up to Julius Roycroft.

Jack Carver had never been more afraid in his life.

DI Sally Speckle hated the cloying sweet dankness of Cobley Wood. The fetid air stuck in her throat and clogged her nostrils. Open spaces were more to her liking. The present rainy spell had come at the end of a gloriously sunny July and early August, and therefore the rain now gave the undergrowth a pungency that it would not have had had the summer been traditionally English. The almost non-stop downpour of the last couple of days had given way to bright spells and showers. Thunder rumbled in the distance, and the far sky was lit by brief flashes of lightning, like diamonds being scattered on a dark cloth.

By the time Speckle and Lukeson reached Cobley Wood, Alec Balson had completed his examination of the woman's body and was placing plastic bags over the victim's head, hands and feet, to preserve any trace evidence.

'DI Harry Barter.' A tall, gaunt man with a raking smoker's cough introduced himself. 'Brigham CID. Dispatched before the powers in the Ivory Tower decided that this lot should be yours. Just thought I'd hold the fort until you arrived.'

'DI Sally Speckle. DS—'

'Hello, Andy,' Barter greeted Lukeson, cutting across

Speckle. 'Still trying to learn the saxophone, are you?'

'I have a go now and then, Harry,' Lukeson said. 'But somehow, I don't think I have the fingers for it.'

'Stick to the piano. The notes are always in the same place, me old son. There's a name written on the underside of the rucksack flap – Brenda Collins. Might not be her name, of course; maybe she nicked the rucksack.' He glanced around. 'The killer seems to have left a shitload of evidence lying about. Sorry.' His apology to Speckle was perfunctory. 'Of course a lot of it could be the leavings of walkers and joggers. The wood is popular with their kind.'

DI Harry Barter's face curled sourly. Obviously his view of walkers and joggers was not very high. Not one for such a carry-on himself, Speckle reckoned.

'As always, the problem will be sifting the wheat from the chaff, eh? Thank heaven high summer has passed. No picnickers swarming all over the place.' Barter became thoughtful. 'You know, if the wagonload of trace evidence belongs to the killer, it looks to me like the killer doesn't give a toss if he's caught.' He turned up the collar of his overcoat. 'Leave it to you lot, then. Welcome, I'm sure. Like I said, try the piano, Andy.' He nodded at Speckle and shot Lukeson a *poor bastard* look before taking his leave.

Sally Speckle looked with pity at the battered woman, her skull caved in. 'We'll have to get an E-FIT for the media, Andy. In the hope that we can get a positive ID. Can't show them that kind of carnage. Like Barter said, she might have stolen the rucksack.'

She turned her attention to Alec Balson, who was supervising the laying of the body on a clean sheet prior to removal. When the body was removed the examination for trace evidence on the ground under the body would begin immediately. A sudden flash from the photographer's camera reflected off Balson's steel-frame glasses and gave his face a sinister, cruel appearance. Knowing the police surgeon to be a kindly and affable man, the fleeting image disturbed Sally Speckle.

'Same MO. Same weapon,' Balson stated the worrisome obvious. 'But maybe not the same killer. Tettle's killer was a left-hander—'

'Or he'd like us to think he was,' Lukeson said.

'That's for you lot to figure out.' Balson grunted. 'But this piece of handiwork is most definitely the work of a right-hander. And no multiple blows. Just one great whack. Dead a couple of hours. No recent sexual activity. Bruising on the inside of her right thigh. But, as I understand it, the man you're looking for picked her up in a nearby pub.' He looked about at the dank and dripping wood. 'Brought her here. Probably a working girl.'

'These might be interesting, ma'am.' The exhibits officer held up an evidence bag containing a sodden tissue with several hairs stuck to it. 'Dark, going grey. Matches the description of the man who picked up the victim.'

'Could also be the same hairs as those found on Anne Tettle's jumper,' Lukeson observed.

'What might the killer's motive be, Andy?' Speckle wondered. 'A hatred of lesbians, maybe?'

'We don't know that the second victim was lesbian. Looks like she was a prostitute.'

'Whore by profession. Lesbian by choice, maybe?'

'If she was lesbian, it's a bit of a coincidence that our lesbian-hating killer found two to murder in such a short period of time, wouldn't you say?'

'Not if Tettle and Collins knew each other.'

'When we have an E-FIT we can check with the residents of the Cecil Street house. If Collins called on Tettle, some-one might have seen her.'

'Don't hold your breath,' Speckle snorted.

Jack Carver sat rigid on the edge of the bed in his hotel room, every nerve-end jangling. The sound of a siren had him racing to the window. He was relieved to see the squad car speed past. But how long would it take for the police to run him to ground? Had anyone at the Coach and Four pub overheard him tell Brenda Collins that he was coming to Brigham? That he was in mortgages? He had to get out of Brigham, and fast.

CHAPTER SEVEN

'Mr Simon Burke?'

'Yes, Officer,' the man who had answered DS Andy Lukeson's summons confirmed, in a voice just a notch above a whisper, edgily glancing back over his shoulder as he spoke.

'Officer?' Sally Speckle pounced. 'How did you know—?'

'You look like police officers,' Simon Burke interjected hastily.

'Did Ms Chambers warn you of our impending arrival, sir?' the DI enquired sternly.

'Yes,' he admitted, downcast. He laughed nervously. 'Oh, you think Alice and I cooked up some cock-and-bull story, is that it?'

'Why would you want to do that?' Andy Lukeson asked.

'We wouldn't. There's no need.'

'You seem tense, sir.'

'You're the police. Everyone gets tense round the police, don't they?'

'Who is it, darling?' a woman called out from inside the house.

'Business associates, dear,' Burke called back, his anxiety reaching new heights.

'Then don't leave them standing on the doorstep.'

A woman's footsteps sounded on the parquet hall floor.

'Look, this is rather awkward,' Burke said in an urgent whisper. 'Alice said she explained the situation. My wife doesn't need to know. Please,' he pleaded.

A woman, a couple of years older, but much more glamorous than Alice Chambers, came to the door. 'Do come in. You'll catch your death standing there.'

Behind her, Simon Burke's face was a mask of pleading.

'That's very kind of you, Mrs Burke,' Andy Lukeson said.

'Why don't we talk in here?' Burke suggested, hurrying ahead to throw open a door which led into his study.

'Would you like me to bring some refreshments? A drink, perhaps?'

'No, thanks, Mrs Burke,' Lukeson responded.

Sally Speckle almost put her foot in it with the standard: *We're on duty.*

'They won't be staying long, dear,' Burke said. 'Run along. You'll miss that new reality thing on telly. The one about celebrities running a pig farm,' he explained condescendingly to Speckle and Lukeson.

Excluded, Betty Burke looked about her like an actress seeking to make an exit after forgetting her lines and the prompt having fallen asleep.

'Thanks anyway, Mrs Burke,' Andy Lukeson said.

'Well, if you change your mind. . . .'

Betty Burke drifted away. Simon Burke hastily ushered Sally Speckle and Andy Lukeson into the study. He closed the door quickly and with great relief.

'Look,' he began urgently. 'I'm not proud of having an affair with my wife's sister, but these things happen, don't they?'

'Your personal life is no concern of ours, sir,' Sally Speckle said, coldly. 'I'm Detective Inspector Speckle and this is Detective Sergeant Lukeson.' Sally Speckle had taken an instant dislike to Simon Burke. He was, she reckoned, the kind of neanderthal who saw only one possible use for a woman. 'What time did you arrive at Ms Chambers flat last evening?'

'Sixish.'

'Did you see anyone who didn't belong? Out of place? Odd?'

'In the house, you mean?'

'Or on the street.'

'No. Neither.'

'Anything unusual, then?'

'No, Inspector. Nothing.'

'Was Ms Chambers at home when you arrived?'

'No, actually.'

'That seems to have come as a surprise to you?' Lukeson said, picking up the questioning.

'That she'd be late, yes. Alice is very prompt. Reliable. Bit of a stickler for routine. Predictable,' he finished, as if he found that quality tiresome. The way he might find loyalty tiresome, Speckle thought. 'Alice phoned me at the office to tell me she'd be late.'

'Did she say why she'd be late?'

'No.'

'And you didn't ask?'

'No.'

'Did she say where she had been when she arrived home?'

'Again, no. And I didn't ask. Alice can get touchy. Has this thing about being owned, as she'd put it. Independent type, Alice.'

'Can you say if Ms Tettle was at home when you arrived?' Speckle asked.

'No way of knowing.'

'I thought perhaps you might have heard music or the telly from her flat? Seen a light under the door? That kind of thing.'

'Anne Tettle was a church mouse type of person, Inspector. Alice said she spent most of her time on the internet.'

'The internet?' Speckle pounced. 'There was no computer in her flat.'

'If there wasn't, someone must have taken it. Her killer, perhaps?' Burke suggested.

'A bit risky. Someone carrying a computer might attract attention.'

'It wasn't a desktop. A laptop. Featherweight and no bigger than. . . .' He drew a square in the air as if finding it necessary to demonstrate what a laptop was to the plodders.

'You've been in Ms Tettle's flat, then, sir?' Lukeson questioned.

'Once. Perhaps twice.'

'In Ms Chambers company?'

'My visits, if one could really call them visits, were more a popping of the head in the door kind of thing.'

'And last evening. Did you pop your head in the door?'

'No. If I had I'd have been able to answer your question about Anne being at home, wouldn't I, Sergeant?'

A point scored. Simon Burke was chuffed.

'How's the tooth, sir?' Lukeson enquired.

'Tooth?'

'Ms Chambers told us that you had to pop out to the chemist last evening for some paracetamol for a nagging tooth.'

'Oh, tooth, yes. Fine.'

'What time would that have been, sir?'

'Six-thirty. Thereabouts.'

'And what chemist did you go to?'

'The one on Bilberry Street.'

'Hatcher's.'

'Yes, that's it. Hatcher's.'

'You'll have a receipt then?'

'No. Tossed it away.'

'That is a pity, sir,' Andy Lukeson said, deadpan. 'But I expect someone at Hatcher's will recall. And if not, Hatcher's will have CCTV footage. A must for chemists nowadays.'

'Don't you believe me?' Burke blustered. 'Why should I lie?'

'Why indeed, sir,' the DS intoned, neutrally. 'It's just that in a murder inquiry every little detail has to be checked, you understand.' He shook his head. 'Pity you didn't keep the receipt, it would have saved a lot of trouble. But I'm sure that with a little effort' – Lukeson was pleased to see the beginnings of a creeping grey pallor on Burke's face – 'we'll be able to establish your presence at Hatcher's readily enough.'

Perspiration glistened on Simon Burke's forehead.

'OK. Look, the chemist bit was a . . . a . . .'

'Lie?' Lukeson said. 'So where were you, if you were not at the chemist?'

'Went to get a breath of air.'

'In a downpour.'

'I often walk in the rain, Sergeant.'

'I see. Well then, that settles that, doesn't it.' Lukeson said, as if satisfied, and gave Burke a moment to think he was out of the woods, before: 'So why did you concoct a story about having gone to the chemist? Why not simply tell Ms Chambers that you had gone for a walk?'

'She'd think I was daft.'

'A long walk, was it? Or a very short walk?' The perspiration on Simon Burke's forehead thickened. He suddenly looked like a trapped animal aware of its inevitable fate as the hunter approached. 'And exceptionally dry,' the DS added. 'Popped your head in, did you, sir?'

Rumbled, Simon Burke's explanation came in a flood. 'It was just a neighbourly call. Quite innocent. Anne kindly offered me a drink, and then I left. Couldn't be more than ten minutes in all.'

'Sounds quite social.'

'It was.'

'Of course your account of events cannot be checked, seeing that Ms Tettle is dead.'

'Why would you doubt me?' Burke asked petulantly.

'Well, you've already lied, sir. Might you not be lying again? Sure nothing out of the ordinary happened?'

'What are you suggesting? What do you mean, out of the ordinary?'

Andy Lukeson held Burke's gaze in a manner he had perfected over the years; a manner which suggested that he might know more than he did. And, as many times before, the ploy worked. Simon Burke's prominent Adam's apple bobbbed.

'She was a bloody lesbo, for God's sake!' he reacted angrily. Lukeson waited, maintaining his inscrutable gaze. 'It was just a peck on the cheek. Nothing to bring down the house about.'

'Is that what Ms Tettle threatened to do? Bring down the house?'

'No. Just a figure of speech.'

'You must have felt foolish.' Speckle said. 'Upset?'

'No.'

'Rejected?'

'No.'

'Perhaps Ms Tettle threatened to tell Ms Chambers?'

'No.'

'Even the police?'

'For a peck on the cheek?'

'Again, unfortunately Ms Tettle cannot verify or contradict your version of events.'

'Oh, I see,' Burke ranted. 'Tettle threatens. I react. Is that it?' His laughter was forced. 'That's utter nonsense.'

'You spent the night with Ms Chambers?' Lukeson asked.

'Yes.'

'You were present this morning when Ms Chambers found Ms Tettle's body.'

'Not for long.'

'Meaning?'

'While I was getting dressed, Alice went to call Tettle. For some unfathomable reason they go to the market every Saturday morning. What Alice had in common with a woman like her, I'll never understand. Alice couldn't wake Tettle, so she came back to the flat to get the spare key to Tettle's flat. When she found the body, I got out fast.'

'I'll be blunt, sir. You were with the murdered woman. Your actions might have precipitated a confrontation—'

'Rubbish!'

'—a confrontation that might have ended in Ms Tettle's death.'

'I told you. I had a drink and left. Nothing happened!'

'And you left the scene of a crime.'

'A crime that had nothing to do with me, Inspector.'

'Would you be willing to give a DNA sample, Mr Burke?'

'Certainly not!'

'We may have to insist,' the DI said.

'I did not murder Anne Tettle,' Burke asserted.

'What do you think?' Speckle asked Lukeson, getting into the car. 'Is Burke our killer?'

'I think Burke is a bit of a tosser. But I'm not sure he has the bottle for murder.'

'Maybe anger or fear or panic gave him the bottle. Burke says that it was a peck on the cheek. But maybe it was a whole lot more serious, like attempted rape or sexual assault. Something that, if he were convicted of it, would put Burke inside for a long time.'

'What if Chambers got home earlier than expected?' Lukeson proposed. 'Tettle's given Burke the heave-ho. He's gone off for a walk to cool down. Tettle tells Chambers that Burke's tried it on and that she's going to the police. Chambers acts to protect Burke and kills Tettle to silence her.'

'Would Alice Chambers really commit murder to protect Burke?' Sally Speckle wondered.

Lukeson reasoned. 'Alice Chambers is in her late thirties to early forties, and she's having an affair with her brother-in-law. That could be the sign of a desperate woman. Or a totally besotted one.'

'And Collins's murder? Where does that fit in to all of this, Andy? Because I just can't believe that there are two like-minded killers, who just happened to pop up at exactly the same time.'

'Without a positive ID, we don't actually know she's Collins yet,' Lukeson reminded Speckle.

'Splitting hairs, Andy. For operational reasons, she's Collins until we know otherwise.' The DI became thought-ful. 'What if I'm wrong? And there are two killers with a common purpose? And what if Tettle and Collins knew each other? And after Tettle's death, Collins, for some reason became a danger to the killer and had to be got rid of?'

'Well, if you're figuring Chambers for Tettle's murder, she has a perfect alibi for when Collins was topped. She was being interviewed by the police.'

'But Burke was free to murder Collins with the weapon Chambers passed on to him. Two killers, one purpose. Same murder weapon.'

Speckle punched out a number on her mobile. 'Anne, did you get a signed statement from Alice Chambers?' When the answer came positive from WPC Fenning, the DI enquired, 'Can you recall which hand Chambers signed the statement with?' There was a long pause. Then: 'Sure? Interesting. Very interesting, indeed.

'Chambers is a left-hander,' she told Lukeson. 'Tettle was the first to be murdered, killed by a left-handed killer. Now while Chambers is being interviewed by the police, Simon Burke, using the same murder weapon and the same MO goes on his merry way to tie up a loose end – Brenda Collins – the intention being to have us looking for a double murderer, only in the tension and confusion, the need to have both women killed by a left-handed killer to achieve this deception is overlooked and Burke beats Collins's brains out with his right hand.'

'What do you think, Andy?'

'Plausible.'

'I sense a *but*.'

'Well, if Chambers is naturally left-handed, it would mean that her left hand was the stronger one, so why the mulitiple and weak blows to Tettle? Why not, as in Collins's case, just one great whack delivered by a naturally right-handed killer? So the idea that the multiple and weak blows were because Tettle's killer was not naturally left-handed and the murderer did not want to risk changing hands because of a possible fight-back by Tettle goes right out of the window. Which rules Chambers out for Tettle's murder, doesn't it?

'There is another theory that fits rather well,' Lukeson said thoughtfully. 'And that is, that Burke, assuming that he is a right-hander, which statistically is very probable, murdered both Tettle and Collins. That would explain the multiple and weaker blows to Tettle, and the need to not risk changing hands during the bludgeoning, because he's a natural right-hander.'

After a thoughtful moment, Sally Speckle grinned. 'Go to the top of the class, Sergeant.'

'Only one problem with all of this,' Lukeson said. 'We haven't a scintilla of proof.'

'Then, we'd better find some, hadn't we?' said Sally Speckle determinedly. 'Let's begin with a search of Chambers' flat and Burke's house.'

CHAPTER EIGHT

'Your first, is it?' a colleague was saying to Mattie Clark as Jack Carver stepped from the lift to put in a brief appearance before quietly slipping away. 'Drives beautifully, does the Almera.'

Almera!

The word rang clarion clear inside Carver's head. Mattie Clark had an Almera!

'Might have got another colour though,' said Clark reflectively. 'Never much fancied white. But white was on special offer.'

White!

There was a ball in Carver's throat which he was finding difficult to swallow. Had it been Mattie Clark parked in Cobley Wood? Coincidence, surely? There had to be thousands of white Almeras. Mattie Clark would have come from the north and would have passed nowhere near Cobley Wood on her way to Brigham.

Jack Carver's relief was brief.

'You nearly scrapped it, you know,' she said, turning to

Carver. 'Turning in to that pub at the last second.'

The words bored into Carver's brain.

'I was down in London to see a friend. Can't take the pill. Did it once without a rubber and now she's banged up and in the most frightful state.' Knowing the state of play between Carver and Clark, their colleague drifted away. Mattie Clark looked closely at Carver. 'You look like shit, Jack.'

He felt a whole lot worse than he looked.

How well did he know Mattie Clark? Not at all, he realized. Their relationship had been purely carnal. The silence between them was reaching a point where Mattie Clark was getting curious.

'Roycroft likes Chanel, does he?' Carver said, to break the impasse.

'Asshole! You had your chance, Jack. What's gotten into you anyway? You took off like a scalded cat from the bar earlier.' She studied him closely. 'Did you see that hitch-hiker on the road this morning? The one who was murdered in Cobley Wood?'

'Hitch-hiker?' Carver hedged.

'You must have. I passed her just before I came to the pub you turned into. She was soaked through. Must have been hitching for an age.' Jack Carver shook his head as convincingly as he could. 'The police are looking for some man who picked her up in the pub,' she added, eyes boring into Carver.

'Matilda, my dear.' Three cheers for good old Julius Roycroft. 'Drinkie?'

'We've got to talk, Jack,' said Mattie Clark, steel behind

the flashing smile she gave Roycroft.

What had Mattie Clark meant by: *We've got to talk?* Talk about what? About him being the man the police were looking for? Or about him leaving Mel? There was no comfort to be gleaned from either possibility. He recalled with a shudder their last fiery parting.

'It's her or me, Jack,' Mattie Clark had warned. 'Can't have your cake and eat it, much as you'd like that.' A heated exhange had ensued followed by the inevitable kiss-and-make-up. Then, drowsily, she had whispered in his ear. 'I'd kill for you, Jack.'

The words echoed back to Carver, and he shuddered. Had Mattie Clark killed for him? And if she had, would she do so again?

Was Mel in danger?

Letitia Gerrard, the proprietor and matron of the Loston Hospice was unwelcoming. 'I'm not sure why you're here,' she told Andy Lukeson. 'Anne Tettle worked for me, and that's really all I can tell you. This whole episode is most inconvenient,' she complained. 'Do you realize how much work goes in to administering a hospice?' Gerrard's tone was that of a teacher seeking an answer from a particularly dense pupil. 'Most unhappy sort, Tettle. Bit of a wet blanket. Not exactly what's required in a hospice. In fact I was thinking of letting her go. But it's so hard to find workers these days.'

In Letitia Gerrard's case, slaves, Lukeson thought.

'Do you know why she was unhappy?'

'I was her employer, not her guardian angel. She was a

Londoner. I expect she found it rather dull here. I suppose if she had a friend, that I know of, it would be Jen Roberts.'

'Ms Roberts was close to Anne Tettle, then?'

'I'm not sure I'd use close to describe their relationship. They chatted affably when they met here at the hospice. In fact I saw them talking to each other last evening. Jen was here to discuss rejoining my *adopt a patient scheme*. An idea I had some time ago, whereby—'

'Yes,' Lukeson interjected, sensing a lengthy blowing of trumpets. Ms Gerrard was obviously irritated by his intervention. 'Ms Roberts told us about your adopt a patient scheme. Quite admirable,' he added, by way of repairing bridges.

'You'd be surprised how many elderly people are off-loaded by their relatives to places like this.' Gerrard's beady eye on him said more forcefully than any words could: *your type*. 'Arthur Granger, the man adopted by Jen Roberts, was one such person. Signed in here five months ago by a nephew whom he never saw again. When he passed away, Jen was beside herself with grief. She had become quite attached to him. There is always that danger, of course.'

Letitia Gerrard sighed.

'I do hope I can persuade her to continue. She is so good with the sick. I have no doubt at all that her visits to Arthur Granger prolonged his life. Terminal cancer, you know.'

'What time was Ms Roberts here last evening?'

'About five. Jen's leaving it so late to call was an inconvenience,' she complained, in the manner only those concerned about their own welfare, irrespective of other people's troubles, do. 'But I suppose it might have had some benefit. She stayed for almost two hours with Mrs Clancy. Poor thing hasn't long to go, I fear. Sleeps most of the time now. I'm hoping that Jen will adopt her. She is quite alone. Her son lives in California.'

'What time did Ms Roberts leave?'

'Seven thirty.'

'You're very precise.'

'I remember, I was settling down to watch *Coronation Street* when Jen phoned me.' Lukeson was genuinely surprised. Even with a leap of imagination he would not have thought the starchy and snobbish hospice matron would have been a *Corrie* fan. 'She was worried that Mrs Clancy was restless. That she'd like it if I came and had a look at her, before she left. I told her rather brusquely, regrettably, to find a nurse. Hope it doesn't prevent her rejoining my scheme. But it was most inconsiderate of her. She knows very well that watching *Coronation Street* for me, is a must.'

'Would that not have been what she should have done in the first place? Summoned a nurse?'

'I suppose she thought that my presence was warranted. The experienced hand, you know. People sometimes forget that I can't be everywhere.'

'And Ms Roberts contacted Nurse. . . ?'

'Walsh.'

'Might I check with Nurse Walsh?'

'Is that necessary, Sergeant?' Gerrard groused. 'Nurse Walsh will be rather busy, you know.'

'I'm sure it won't disrupt her routine too much.'

'Oh, very well.' Gerrard picked up the phone and punched out an extension number. 'Susan, is Nurse Walsh with you? Good. Please ask her to come to the phone.' She handed the phone to Lukeson who, after a moment enquired, 'Nurse Walsh? Sorry to disturb you. Sergeant Andy Lukeson, Loston CID here.' He paused and listened for a moment. 'No, I'm not calling about your fine for parking on double yellow lines. I believe you were summoned to a patient last evening by Jen Roberts. Is that so?' A moment, then: 'Thank you.'

'Is that all?' Gerrard enquired.

It was not a question, rather a dismissal.

On opening the door of her flat, Alice Chambers looked curiously at Andy Lukeson who was accompanied by DC Helen Rochester, two PCs and a WPC. 'Search my flat?' she exclaimed on being shown the search warrant by Lukeson. She watched aghast as the search team went past her into the flat.

Taking advantage of her astonishment, Lukeson questioned: 'Where were you between leaving work and arriving home last evening, Ms Chambers?'

'Is that any of your business?'

'This is a murder inquiry,' he stated bluntly. 'And until it's solved, everything is my business.'

Alice Chambers looked quickly away.

'I was meeting someone, Sergeant,' she said at last, in a hushed voice.

'Someone?'

'A man.'

69

'And this man's name?'

'Don't know who he is, or where he is.' Alice Chambers' shoulders drooped. 'I met him on a chatroom. Stupid bloody carry-on, I know. But I was curious, you see. I was to meet him outside the Plaza cinema. He didn't turn up. I realize now, of course, how terribly foolish I'd been. I could have been meeting any kind of crank or crackpot.'

'Has this man made contact since?'

'I don't want to know. You don't have to mention any of this to Simon, do you?' She shook her head. 'All the trouble I went to. Silly me. And all for nothing, too.' Her face curled in distaste. 'Changing clothes in a public loo. You see, I didn't want the man I was meeting to know where I worked. So I changed out of my Labatt's uniform, put it in a supermarket shopping bag, concealed under some groceries. I was like a bloody spy.

'Then, later, I changed back. I put the wet clothes I'd been wearing into the plastic bag and put my uniform back on, so that Simon would not wonder why I had changed clothes, you understand. I needn't have bothered. Simon was not here when I got home. Walked to the chemist. Nagging tooth, remember?'

What a clever girl you are, Andy Lukeson thought.

'Something come to mind?' he enquired, when Alice Chambers' brow furrowed.

'Oh, it's nothing, Sergeant.'

Lukeson waited, giving Chambers time to fully consider whatever it was that was bothering her. Eventually she said: 'Funny, thing. Simon was perfectly dry when he arrived back. Just a few drops on his overcoat.'

'Probably a dry patch,' Lukeson said, casually dismissive, hoping to steer Chambers away from realizing the significance of what she had just told him. *Perfectly dry.* Burke would be, if he'd only crossed over from Anne Tettle's flat. 'Wet clothes must be a problem in a flat?'

'Oh, I usually bung them off to the laundrette or dry cleaners.'

'Usually?'

'Yes. But last night I just slung them in the washing machine and then into the drier.'

Might it be that she could not send bloodstained clothes to the launderette or dry cleaners? An officer searching a desk pulled out a drawer too far and its contents scattered all over the floor.

'For God's sake be careful,' Chambers rebuked the PC, and enquired of Lukeson in the same breath, 'What exactly are you expecting to find, Sergeant?'

Lukeson fell back on an old and well-tried police ploy. 'Just routine, Ms Chambers.'

'Routine?' She bristled with anger. 'I'm not an idiot, don't treat me like one.' Andy Lukeson had formed the opinion in the last couple of minutes that Alice Chambers was very far from being an idiot. 'The next time I'll find a body I'll look the other way.'

Then she held Andy Lukeson's gaze.

'Oh, shit! You think I murdered Anne Tettle, don't you?'

Lukeson went downstairs with one thought uppermost in his mind. What if the man from the chatroom had indeed turned up and had followed Alice Chambers home? And, maybe, thwarted by Simon Burke's arrival back had changed course for Anne Tettle's flat? But how might he have got past the digital access code to gain entry to the house? By simply pretending to arrive at the same time as someone else about to enter the building, perhaps?

'Ask round the other flats if anyone let a stranger into the house,' Lukeson instructed Rochester. 'A bloke who might have turned up on the doorstep just as they were coming in, maybe.'

'Are you thinking that the chatroom Romeo might have followed Chambers home, Sarge?' Rochester asked shrewdly.

'You have good ears, DC Rochester,' he said, indulgently. 'The thought had crossed my mind. And don't confine it to a man. Computer chatrooms can be pretty weird places. Women are not the gentle and innocent creatures they used to be.'

'You believe her then? The chatroom story, I mean?'

'I'm not sure what or who I believe at this point,' he replied.

Lukeson checked his notebook for Simon Burke's telephone number. Burke answered on the second ring.

'Sergeant Lukeson of Loston CI—'

'Yes?' Burke sounded on edge.

'Where were you this morning, say between nine and eleven o'clock, sir?'

'Walking on the downs for most of it. I needed the exercise after what had happened.'

'Alone?'

'Quite alone.'

'Like walking, do you?'

'Yes,' Burke answered curtly, in response to the note of sarcasm in Lukeson's voice.

'It was raining rather heavily this morning. Do you always walk in the rain?'

'It can be quite refreshing.'

'Did anyone see you?'

'Not that I know of. That's what's so refreshing about walking in the rain. Not many about.'

'Did you see anyone, then?'

'No.'

'Come home perfectly dry, did you, sir? Like after your supposed walk in the rain last night to the chemist.'

There was a long silence.

'OK,' Burke said, quietly fearful. 'I didn't go for a walk last evening, Sergeant. I simply went out to my car to make a phone call.'

'Why didn't you just say so when first questioned?'

'I had my reasons. The call was to a lady. It's all rather delicate, Sergeant. You see, I've become involved with someone else. The lady in question doesn't know about Alice. And, of course, Alice doesn't know about her.'

What an absolute shit you are, Lukeson thought.

'I'll need this woman's name and address,' Lukeson said, not bothering to conceal his contempt for Burke.

'If the police were to call round, it could be rather difficult.'

'Well, it's something you'll have to work out between you all,' Lukeson barked.

A long defeated sigh came down the line. 'Her name is

Cecily Hampton.' Burke added her address.

'Did you see Ms Chambers come home last night?'

'No.'

'Where were you parked?'

'Just across the street.'

'So had she come home, you would have seen her?'

'Not necessarily.'

'But more than likely, you would have?' Lukeson pressed.

'I suppose.'

'But she was at home when you arrived back inside?'

'Yes.'

'How long were you outside for?'

'Twenty minutes, give or take. I needed to gather my wits before facing Alice.'

'And did you check before you came out to make the phone call, to see if Ms Chambers was at home?'

'No. When I left Anne Tettle I went straight out to my car. I needed to call Cecily right away.'

'Can you recall whether the washing machine was on when you arrived back at the flat?' Lukeson enquired.

'What an odd question. Yes. It was, actually. The machine is old. Makes the most awful racket.'

Twenty minutes. Enough time for Chambers to have gone to Tettle's flat? Commit murder? And be washing her bloodstained clothes when Burke returned? Needs must made a lot of things possible, Andy Lukeson concluded.

'Of what significance can it be whether the washing machine was on or off, Sergeant?'

'Goodbye, Mr Burke.'

'You will try and be discreet with Ms Hampton, won't you?'

DS Andy Lukeson gave Simon Burke no comfort. Discretion and murder were not compatible.

CHAPTER NINE

"Police have again appealed to the man who left the Coach and Four public house with the murdered woman to come forward.' Mel Carver, waiting for a repeat of *Fawlty Towers* to begin, sat casually looking at pictures of Cobley Wood, where a woman's body had been found earlier that day. In the background, the Scene of Crime Officers were going about their gruesome task of gathering evidence. 'Cobley Wood is a popular picnic and recreational area between Loston and Brigham.'

Mel sat up. Jack would have passed Cobley Wood.

'Police are appealing to anyone who was in Cobley Wood or the general area this morning between nine and eleven to come forward. Detective Inspector Sally Speckle of Loston CID is leading the hunt for the killer, and is anxious to remind viewers that even though they may feel that any information they have is of no importance, it may very well be vital.'

The camera angle widened to bring Sally Speckle into shot.

'How soon do you think the police will catch this danger-ous killer, Inspector?' Jeff Hornby asked in his familiar clipped way.

'We're fully confident that with the help of the public—'

'How soon, Inspector?' the reporter interjected aggres-sively.

'This enquiry is at a very early stage, Mr Hornby. Right now we are asking for the public's help. The dead woman was a hitch-hiker, so she may have been seen getting a lift. Or perhaps someone saw a woman in a car in the wood, possibly a maroon Vauxhall Vectra. But really any car. So please, if you were in or near Cobley Wood today, give the Cobley Wood incident room a call. Or for that matter any police station.'

'Is the man who left the Coach and Four pub with the murdered woman the chief suspect, Inspector?'

'The police are pursuing several lines of inquiry. We only need to talk to this man. Our appeal in no way implies guilt.'

'And you have a description of this man for our viewers.'

'Yes. He's—'

Mel Carver's breath caught in her throat as DI Sally Speckle described a man who could be her husband.

'Is there a link between this woman's murder and the murder in Loston yesterday?'

'At this time any talk of a link between the women's deaths would be purely speculative.'

Jeff Hornby raised an eyebrow. 'Two women. Only miles apart. More or less the same age. Brutally bludgeoned to death with a hammer. I put it to you, Inspector, that there's no maybe about it,' the reporter stated bluntly.

Sally Speckle was taken aback by the degree of Hornby's knowledge. For operational reasons, how the victims had died had not been made public. Which meant that there had been loose talk. Or, more sinisterly, Hornby had an informant in the police – in fact on the murder team. An insider passing on information for, no doubt, an appropriate fee. She hoped that the camera had been kind, and had not shown her surprise as starkly as she had felt it. Right now if she had within her grasp whoever had passed on information, by mistake or by intent, she would skin them alive.

Hornby went for the jugular.

'Should women be locking their doors, Inspector?'

'It would, of course, until the police catch this killer, be wise for everyone to be careful,' she stated tersely, coming across as peeved.

'Rumour has it that the woman murdered in Loston was gay. Might that be the link between the women?'

'No comment.'

Hornby tipped the side of his nose. 'Of course.' He went for the jugular again. 'Inspector. It looks as though we have a serial killer on the loose.' Before Sally Speckle could respond, the reporter turned to the camera. 'Jeff Hornby at Cobley Wood.'

Hornby stepped out of shot and drew a line across his throat to cut the transmission.

'Thank you, Inspector,' he said amiably. 'That was a very good interview.'

It certainly had been from his point of view.

The phone number of the Cobley Wood and Loston incident rooms appeared on screen. Then the newscaster came back on screen.

'The threatened rail strike for next week may now be called off. . . .'

The sound of beating drums in Mel Carver's ears drowned out everything.

Jack Carver was back in his room, reeling, trying desperately to shut out the idea that Mattie Clark might have murdered Brenda Collins. He had just seen the flashpoint jealousy that Mattie Clark was capable of. Had the carefree roll in the hay arrangement they had had, suddenly become an obsession, the stuff of nightmares? Might she, having seen him with Brenda Collins, lashed out? But why would Mattie Clark wait in Cobley Wood in the first place? Could it be that she had pulled in there to wait for him to come along? He knew she was impulsivly mischievous. He recalled having told her about a forthcoming weekend trip to Paris with Mel the previous year. Mattie Clark had turned up at the same hotel. It had been her idea of a surprise. Mattie had come to their room while Mel was in the shower. 'Let's do it right now, Jack,' she had said, pulling him to the floor. 'It'll be the best ever.' He had made faint protests about it being madness, but once on the floor with Mattie Clark on top of him, he could not have cared less. The tryst had lasted only minutes, but it had been the most intense sex he had ever had. 'Sometimes it's better if you don't plan it,' Mattie had said, slipping out of the room just as the door of the *en suite* began to open. So an impromptu tryst in Cobley Wood might very well have appealed to her.

The possibility stunned Jack Carver.

There was no denying that Mattie Clark had become more possessive, but had she also become more obsessive?

'There's a lot of Vectras,' said PC Roger Bennett, replying to DI Sally Speckle's question at the briefing in a complaining tone of voice that indicated his displeasure at still being a PC twelve years after joining the force; a displeasure that, Speckle was sure, was all the more pronounced at having a graddie as a guv'nor. 'Take time, won't it.'

'We're working flat out, ma'am,' said WPC Sue Blake, Bennett's partner, quick to pour oil on what were potentially troubled waters. Blake's attitude was the complete opposite to Bennett's. After only two years' service, she was still confident that one day she would be the Chief Constable and that in the not too distant future.

Bennett threw Blake a contemptuous look, obviously seeing her intervention as obsequious. Speckle took exception to Bennett's attitude and, later, would not waste any time in letting him know of her displeasure.

'Bad news, I'm afraid.' All eyes turned to Andy Lukeson. 'The car might not even be a Vectra.'

'Bloody typical,' Bennett snorted.

Lukeson went on: 'Fred Clampton, the elderly man who saw Collins and the man leave from the pub window has poor eyesight, even wearing specs. Not very good on colours either, I'm afraid.'

Sally Speckle groaned.

'Uniform recreated the scene. Four different cars were driven out of the pub car park. A maroon Vectra. A red Mondeo. A grey Peugeot and a green Focus. The Focus he described as reddish. The Mondeo was "one of those German cars". And the Vectra became a black Mercedes. He got the make of Peugeot right, but thought it was also black.'

'Bloody Moses!' PC Brian Scuttle exclaimed, and stated the obvious, 'Imagine what the greenest defence QC would make of that lot.'

'What about this mysterious chatroom Johnny who might have followed Alice Chambers home?' DC Charlie Johnson asked Lukeson.

'No one at Cecil Street is admitting to a thing,' Lukeson replied dourly.

'Anything back from the lab on Chambers' clothes?' Helen Rochester enquired.

'Nothing so far,' Sally Speckle said. 'What can there be, anyway, washed as they were?'

'Maybe the clothes are a smokescreen.' All eyes switched to WPC Anne Fenning. 'I was thinking that maybe Chambers directed us to the clothing she had washed – a decoy.'

Under intense scrutiny, Fenning wished that she had kept her mouth shut.

'I mean, what if those clothes are not the clothes she murdered Tettle in? We'd test them and find nothing. While all the time, she had dumped the clothes she was wearing when she murdered Tettle and, thinking we had the right clothes, we wouldn't be looking for them.'

Still the subject of intense scrutiny, she ended:

'It was just a thought.'

'And a devious one at that,' Andy Lukeson said, in a congratulatory manner. 'One well worth thinking about, I'd say.'

'Shouldn't we have searched Simon Burke's house?' WPC Sue Blake asked.

'In hand,' Speckle informed her. 'DC Rochester will be searching Burke's house immediately after this briefing.'

'Burke won't be a happy puppy, will he?' PC Brian Scuttle chuckled. 'The cat will really be out of the bag.'

'Maybe if we threw a scare into the Cecil Street crowd, politely pointing out the danger they might be in if they keep their gobs shut, being in a position to point the finger at a possible murderer, they might not be so bloody smug!'

The strategy was DC Charlie Johnson's.

'Police officers are not supposed to scare people presumed innocent,' Speckle said.

Anne Fenning shifted uneasily in her chair, and confessed, 'I took the liberty of suggesting as much, in the gentlest manner, of course. But if anyone did let a stranger in, they were still not prepared to admit to their gaffe. Probably feel stupid.'

'Better stupid than dead!' Speckle snapped. 'The murder weapon?' This time her question was directed at Lukeson.

'Not found yet.'

'Anything on the man who left the pub with the victim, then?'

'All stops are out,' Lukeson said.

'We're getting nowhere fast!'

'It's early days, guv,' DC Rochester pointed out, bravely in Lukeson's opinion. There were not many junior officers who dared to point out the obvious to a senior.

Speckle glared at her. Rochester was unfazed, and this earned her Sally Speckle's admiration. She wondered whether, in her urgency to prove herself, she was pushing too hard. But what was too hard? Two murders had been committed. Soon would come the lurid headlines, and shortly after the questions from senior officers: questions she would not have answers to, judging by progress to date. And Jeff Hornby's TV interview would not have helped. Inevitably the wisdom of promoting an officer who had not climbed the traditional ladder to promotion, a graddie, would come up for discussion. She already sensed that the real coppers were closely watching how she handled herself, and she had no doubt at all that many were waiting for her to fall flat on her face.

'My money is still on the bloke who picked up Collins,' Charlie Johnson opined.

'For both murders?' Lukeson queried.

Johnson shrugged. 'Two women about the same age, murdered within a couple of miles of each other in a short time, heads bashed in with a hammer. I rest my case.'

'The type of murder weapon has not been confirmed,' Speckle said.

'Balson's never wrong,' Johnson said. 'It's a hammer all right. Two different killers? Who just happened to have offed their victims with a hammer? Never.'

Sally Speckle outlined her and Andy Lukeson's idea about two killers with a common purpose, Burke and

Chambers. And the idea of Burke being the sole murderer. Opinion on their respective worth broke about even between each.

'What about the E-FIT of the man who was seen leaving the pub with Collins?' PC Roger Bennett asked, not really interested, but feeling that he should make a contribution. His main concern was satisfying the illegal bookie to whom he owed money and whom he was to meet in an hour, well short of what the loan shark had demanded as a payment to avoid having serious physical damage inflicted on him.

'Another blank at Cecil Street,' DC Rochester said.

'And the Collins E-FIT?'

'Nothing there either.'

'We're really up against it, aren't we?' was Bennett's wholly unnecessary reminder of the team's lack of progress.

Andy Lukeson had more bad news.

'The man's E-FIT might be more of a hindrance than a help,' he said. 'When it came down to it, each of the witnesses in the pub seems to have seen a different man. Too many witnesses. Best if you have only one or two. That way egos don't come into play and distort the results.

'And the other man who offered Collins a lift. The one who was arrested for being over the limit says he took no notice of what the suspected killer was driving. But his description of the man is nearer what we got first, before the battle of the egos began.'

After a lengthy gaze into the distance, the DI asked Lukeson, 'Do you think the man who picked Collins up in the pub is our killer, Andy?'

'Seems to fit the *bill*, so to speak,' Lukeson said.

The attempt at humour sank like a stone.

'Bloody stupid killer, if you ask me,' said WPC Anne Fenning. 'The way he left trace evidence all over both crime scenes.'

'Panicked,' Helen Rochester opined. 'A picnic area. No time to tidy up. Any second someone could have driven in.'

'Unlikely,' Scuttle said. 'It was bucketing down.'

'We don't have definitive results from the lab yet,' Speckle said. 'A lot of the so-called evidence could be spurious. But we do know that the blood found on Collins's jeans is not hers. So we'll work on the assumption that it's the killer's blood.'

'Has the fingerprinting and DNA of the residents of the Cecil Street house been completed?' Speckle enquired of DC Charlie Johnson.

'All except two.' He checked his notebook. 'A Mr Alfred Cannon and a Miss Judith Croft. A lot of guff about their civil liberties, guv.'

'Did you check for a reason why, other than their concern for their civil liberties, Mr Cannon and Miss Croft might be shy about providing fingerprint and DNA samples?'

'Nothing on Croft. But Cannon's got form. Two convictions. One for shoplifting and one for burglary, for which he did time.'

'Burglary? Maybe Tettle came home and found him in her flat?' the DI speculated. 'Was he asked where he was between five and seven last evening?'

'Says he was visiting an old mate in hospital,' DC

Johnson said. 'A bloke by the man of Frank Carty.'

'Did Carty confirm Cannon's story?'

'Yes. But I wouldn't place too much credence on Cannon's alibi or Carty's truthfulness. Birds of a feather. They shared a cell. They both have a fondness for other people's property.'

'If Cannon really was visiting Carty, someone must have seen him. A nurse? Another patient?'

Johnson shook his head. 'Hospital wards at visiting times are busy places, guv. Everyone concentrates on their visitors. And nurses use visiting times to write up any notes or reports that need updating or writing. Or to simply take a breather.'

'Keep at Carty,' Speckle ordered. 'Nothing on Simon Burke's prints. Has, as far as the law is concerned, led a blameless life. Chambers, ditto. DNA results will take longer. The same old story. Understaffed and overworked.'

Sally Speckle glanced despondently out the rain-washed window. Lukeson sensed in her the need to be striding out. He knew Speckle's fondness for wide open spaces; she often spent her holidays and shorter breaks exploring Dartmoor and other wildernesses like the Scottish Highlands, and sometimes places like the Beara Peninsula in West Cork and the Kerry mountains. 'The man from the Coach and Four could be a bloke who just gave the woman a lift, and is now quietly having a nervous breakdown?' she said, returning her gaze to the officers who made up the murder team.

The idea sank like the proverbial stone.

'He was in a pub and got into a tiff with this other man

who had offered Collins a lift,' Speckle said. 'Would he then, being the centre of attention, blatantly pick up Brenda Collins? And even if he did, would he in fact murder her, after what happened at the Coach and Four?'

'Pick-ups in pubs are a penny a dozen,' Johnson said. 'Part of pub culture. Normally going unnoticed. At the time he picked up Collins he was after a good time. It backfired and he lost it.'

'The Coach and Four is a quiet country pub, not a city fleshpot. And Saturday morning isn't your normal pick-up time, is it?'

'If he's innocent, he'll come forward,' Lukeson said.

'Would you come forward?' Speckle asked. 'Put yourself in a juror's place, as he must have. Man picks up a hitch-hiker, thinking, easy sex—'

Speckle turned her attention to the male officers.

'Now think back. You're driving along. You see a female hitch-hiker. What's any red-blooded male's first reaction?' Gazes were averted. 'The thing is, most men don't push it. And if they get a refusal, they leave it.

'Now. Hitcher gets out of the car. You drive off. Along comes the next bloke. And the next thing you know is that the girl you dropped was given a lift by someone else, has been murdered, and the police are looking for you because someone saw you either pick her up or drop her off.

'What do you do? Risk coming forward and ending up doing life? Or bury your head in the sand and hope that the police will either never find you, or before they do, they'll find the real killer?'

'If you don't come forward and you're caught, then in

court that will be seen as guilt with a capital G,' DC Rochester pointed out.

'But only if you're caught.'

'What if the killer was in the other car?' Scuttle speculated. A snippet of a tyre-tread had been found on soft ground alongside a gravel path under some low hanging trees. 'Whoever was in this car sees what goes on between the man and Collins. For some reason this man leaves Collins behind. Mr B, his blood up, thinks he'll have some of the same, thanks very much. Collins tells him to piss off.'

'What could this Mr B have seen to get his blood up?' Lukeson said. 'Balson says that there was no sexual activity between the man and Collins.'

'But it must have been obvious what they were in Cobley Wood for, mustn't it? So Mr B's imagination goes into overdrive. And it might have been someone from the pub who followed them.'

'Firstly, would Collins, if she was a pro, send this second man packing?' Lukeson speculated. 'Business is business. Secondly, Collins had her head bashed in. That means that Mr B would have to have had a hammer to hand, ready to lash out with. Or he would have had to return to the car and get it. Either way, would Collins hang about?

'And there was no struggle. Which suggests that Collins did not feel threatened.'

'Knew her killer, maybe?' said Sue Blake.

'Or at least saw no danger,' Speckle said.

'I don't know about that,' Anne Fenning contributed. 'Put yourself in Cobley Wood. A dark and dreary day. No one around. A man gets out of a car and comes towards you. You'd be on your guard, spit quick.'

'Assuming it was a man,' Sally Speckle said. 'It might have been a woman.' She looked at Lukeson. 'You toyed with the idea of Tettle having been murdered by a woman, Andy.'

After a brief lull to consider this possibility, WPC Sue Blake was the first to speak. 'I think the man who left the pub with Brenda Collins is as guilty as hell. And when we nab him, I reckon the stack of forensics we have will nail him. Hairs. Fibres. Blood. Footprints. We're bursting at the seams with forensics.'

'That's what worries me,' Andy Lukeson said. 'Even if half of what was found at the scenes of crime is valid evidence, there's way too much of it. It might have been stage-managed.'

'And we might be playing silly buggers,' said DC Charlie Johnson. 'Maybe in the madness of the moment he wasn't even aware of the evidence he'd left? Maybe he panicked and legged it? Or maybe he was counting on the downpour to obliterate it? Remember, the rain stopped quite suddenly, during which time the body was discovered. Had it not stopped raining even for a while longer, there'd be precious little evidence to find. Maybe the bastard was simply unlucky.'

'Have you taken a statement from the man who found the body?' Speckle asked Anne Fenning.

'Yes. Seventy-two years old. A retired vicar. Walks along the same path every day, regular as clockwork.'

'Check him out anyway. Now,' the DI's gaze swept the room, 'before you leave. You'll have seen my interview with Jeff Hornby earlier, during which Hornby displayed an extensive knowledge; knowledge which he could have got only one way. From someone on the murder team. You lot.

'Now, I'd prefer that whoever it is owns up before I have to root him or her out. If that has to be done, I won't go easy on whoever it is. Understood? So save yourself and me a lot of unpleasantness. A lot of heartache. And a ton of grief!'

CHAPTER TEN

'I must speak to my husband right now,' Mel Carver insisted, when the hotel receptionist told her that there was no reply from Jack Carver's room. 'I've been trying his mobile, but it's been constantly powered off.'

'Just a moment. I'll page Mr Carver, madam. *Will Mr Jack Carver please go to courtesy phone two in the hotel foyer, where there is a call waiting for him.*'

'Probably the wife checking up on you, Jack,' one of two colleagues Carver was talking to chuckled. 'So don't sound breathless when you pick up the phone.'

'*Mr Carver to courtesy phone two, please.*'

'Probably the wife wanting to tell you that she's preggers by the milkman and they're doing a runner to live in a shack in the South Seas,' the second man of a duo laughed.

'I'd better . . .' Carver drifted away towards the foyer.

'Wound as tight as a Swiss cuckoo clock, is our Jack,' the first man commented. 'Not like him one little bit.

Jack thrives on these shindigs. Life and soul of the party sort.'

His colleague nodded in Roycroft's direction, whose eyes were taking in the delights of Mattie Clark's generously exposed cleavage.

'Sick as a parrot, our Jack. Kicked out of La Clark's bed for Roycroft. I'd cut the horny old bastard's throat, if I were Jack.'

'There's that, of course, but Jack's not been himself since that incident in the foyer earlier.'

'What was that all about?'

'A case of mistaken identity, Jack says. Bloody hell, I wouldn't like to be the woman Jack mistook that courier for. He was ready to rip her heart out. Had a right go, he did.'

'I'm sorry, madam,' the receptionist was telling Mel Carver. 'Mr Carver is not responding.'

'He's not on life support, is he?' Mel snapped. 'Try again.'

'*If Mr Jack Carver is in the hotel—*'

Carver grabbed the phone. 'This is Jack Carver.'

'It's me, Jack.'

'This is not a very good time, Mel.'

'Phone me back.'

'Like I said—'

'Now, Jack! From some place quiet.'

He hung up and went outside to the hotel car park to phone back.

'I've seen the news,' Mel said.

'News?' he hedged.

'Don't piss around! Did you pick up that woman found murdered in Cobley Wood?' Jack Carver's heart beat like a war drum. 'You did, didn't you.' It was not a question. 'You bastard! Did you—?'

'No!'

'Yes, you did. You knew what I was going to ask.'

'No, I didn't do anything, Mel,' Carver declared vehemently.

'You'll have to go to the police.'

'Don't be daft. They'd lock me up and throw away the key. I didn't kill her, Mel.'

'Then tell them that.'

'Oh, come on,' Carver said, exasperated.

'If you didn't kill her, you have nothing to fear.'

'I wonder how many fools believed that before.'

'What choice do you have?'

'They might never find me, that's the choice I have, Mel.'

'They have an accurate description, and they know that you drive a maroon-coloured Vectra. And you probably left a shitload of evidence in that wood. As sure as night follows day, the police will find you. For God's sake, couldn't you have just kept going!'

'I did. It was pissing rain. I splashed her. I stopped at a pub for coffee and she turned up. I felt I owed her.'

'What had you in mind?' Mel scoffed. 'Drying her clothes in the car?'

'I felt sorry for her.'

'Don't give me that. You haven't a charitable bone in your entire body, Jack Carver. If you had to help Christ with his cross, you'd claim that you had an allergy to thorns!'

'Look, all I did was give her a lift, Mel.'

'*Ride*, don't you mean!'

Jack Carver ignored his wife's jibe. 'I've been thinking—'

'A bit late for that,' Mel interjected scornfully.

'Don't do the bitch, Mel. Just listen. Your sister's place in Devon. . . .'

'Forget it. You know how prissy Janet is about the cottage. She'd never—'

'Know,' Carver interjected.

'And how would that help?'

'I could lie low. Hope the police find the real killer. There's nothing else I can do, Mel,' he pleaded.

'Did anyone see you in Cobley Wood?'

'I'm not sure. I saw a parked car when I was leaving.'

'Make?'

'An Almera.'

'Did you get its registration number?'

'Oh, come on, Mel.'

'Driver, then. Man or woman?'

'It was raining. The windows were fogged up.'

'But there was someone in the car?'

'I think I saw a shape. But I can't be certain.'

'Jack, have you thought that whoever was in that car might be the killer?'

'Of course I bloody have.'

'Then you have to tell the police.'

'No police!'

'When will you leave for Devon?' Mel Carver asked

resignedly, unable to see any other way out of her husband's dilemma, temporary though the respite would be, she reckoned.

'Later. When I can slip away quietly. Everyone is well on the way to getting pissed. I won't be missed.'

'Jack, if you didn't kill her, who did?'

'Someone in the pub, maybe. There was an old duffer from an age when sinners had to be punished. Maybe his punishment for a harlot was death? And there was another man who offered Collins a lift. He didn't take her rejection very well. He left the pub directly after. And there's that nutter Williams.'

'Graham Williams? The man who created stink at the opening of the new branch?'

'An unstable thug of the first order. And there's Lucy Bell. A sacked employee, bearing a grudge. Or maybe her sister? She came round ranting and raving. Lunatic bitch.'

'But they couldn't possibly have known that you'd meet up with this woman, Jack.'

'What if Williams or either of the Bell sisters followed me, Mel?'

'Followed you?' Mel said sceptically. 'That seems improbable. How would they even know where you were going? And there's something else, Jack. Jen came round to tell me that Anne Tettle's been murdered as well.'

'Bloody hell!'

'Two women murdered within miles of each other. You knew one and you were with the other. Creepy, isn't it.'

On his way back to the hotel from the car park, Jack

Carver's heart lurched when he saw the police car parked at the entrance to the hotel. In his panic, he could only see one reason for their presence – his imminent arrest. There was only one thing to do. . . .

Scarper!

Jen Roberts was obviously taken aback on finding DS Andy Lukeson on her doorstep. 'Sorry to trouble you,' he said. 'May I?'

Roberts led the way to the sitting-room.

'I've already given a signed statement,' she said, a little tetchily, pointing to an armchair for Lukeson to sit in.

'Just one or two questions. Do you know if Anne Tettle was in a relationship, Ms Roberts?'

'I wasn't Anne's keeper, Sergeant. But, yes, I thought she might have been.'

Lukeson produced the E-FIT of Brenda Collins. 'Have you seen this woman with Ms Tettle?'

'No,' she said after close scrutiny of the E-FIT. 'Who is she?'

'The woman who was found murdered in Cobley Wood earlier today.'

'Oh, I see. You think that Anne and she were . . . *close*? And their murders might be linked?'

'It's a thought, yes. At this early stage of a murder inquiry, nothing is ruled in or out.'

'Is it true that if you don't catch a murderer in the first couple of days, then you probably won't catch him at all, Sergeant? I read that somewhere.'

'I wouldn't say that, Ms Roberts. But, of course, the

longer the investigation goes on the colder the trail becomes.' He glanced about him. 'Live alone, do you?'

'Yes.' Jen Roberts fixed a steady gaze on Lukeson. 'Unmarried. Not a hint of a man about the place. Knew Anne Tettle. Conclusion. Lesbian, too?' Her gaze hardened. 'I choose to live alone because I like it that way, Sergeant. Am I a suspect?'

'Why would you think that?'

'Well, think about it this way. If I were in a relationship with Anne and I found out that she was cheating on me with the woman murdered in Cobley Wood, I might have gone off the deep end and killed them both.'

'Did you?'

Roberts laughed. 'I might have. If I were lesbian and Anne Tettle's lover. Unfortunately for you and very fortunately for me, neither is true.'

Lukeson walked briskly to the car parked a little way along the street, in which Sally Speckle was waiting, having reasoned that female interviewees responded better to male officers. He was not sure if her reasoning had been very sound. He got into the car and gave his superior the gist of the interview, which really amounted to very little. He yawned. 'Times like this I wish I'd stayed in Traffic.'

'You were in Traffic?'

'Don't make it sound like I had leprosy,' Lukeson protested jokingly. 'I wasn't born a detective genius, you know.'

'Happy there?'

'It was less frantic. I'm finding out that dull and boring has its compensations.'

'Why did you move?'

'I'm not really sure. But I suspect that it was because I had a feeling that I wasn't a real copper.' His brow furrowed. 'All legs and Twiggy thin.'

'What?'

'Helen Rochester's description of Jen Roberts. Tall, for a woman, isn't she?' Lukeson mimicked someone striking downwards with a hammer.

'She has an alibi for the time of Anne Tettle's murder, remember. She was sitting with a patient in Loston Hospice.'

'Pity.'

Lukeson put the car in gear, and was about to drive away when there was a rap on the driver's window. Jen Roberts was holding up a laptop. 'This completely slipped my mind, Sergeant,' she said, when he opened the car door. 'It belonged to Anne Tettle. She lent it to me when I got the ludicrous idea that I'd become a novelist.'

'Thank you.' Lukeson took the laptop and handed it to Speckle. 'We've been wondering where it had got to. How is the novel going?'

'Great first chapter. Then,' she gave a thumbs down, 'fizzled out like a Guy Fawkes firework. I'm afraid I made the grim discovery that an idea is a hell of a long way from being a book.'

'If at first you don't succeed, eh,' Lukeson said.

'Who knows. Maybe. 'Night.'

'Hard to imagine her as a cold-blooded murderer?' Sally Speckle said, looking through the rear window of the car at Roberts.

Lukeson chuckled. 'I'm sure everyone who knew Jack the Ripper probably would have said the same thing.'

Speckle studied Lukeson. 'You're not thinking that Roberts is a double murderer, are you, Andy?'

CHAPTER ELEVEN

Jack Carver was turning back to his car when a colleague hailed him. 'Jack, wait up, old man.' His summoner was Larry Slater, a windbag who spread gossip faster than a force ten gale spreads a bushfire. Two uniformed police officers were with Slater. 'Good evening, sir,' the younger of the pair greeted Carver. 'Just a word, if we may.' Larry Slater hurried away, dodging out of the path of a drunk coming from the hotel to the car park, eager to be the first with the news that the police were interviewing Jack Carver. The older PC stood a little way off in a shadow, no doubt to scrutinize his reactions and weigh up his answers, Carver reckoned. 'It's about an incident you were involved in today, sir.'

Incident?

Such an innocuous description for a brutal murder. It might have been a Friday night dust-up outside a chippie the police had come to talk about. But he supposed that to the police everything was an incident until it became a definite something. Where to begin, that was the problem. But did it matter where he began? There was nowhere he could start that would make a difference. The drunk staggered against the older constable. Car keys clattered to the ground.

'Is it your intention to drive a vehicle, sir?'

'None of your damn bishness,' the man slurred, his mood belligerent.

The sudden interruption acted like an electric shock on Jack Carver. *Incident.* The police were not here about Brenda Collins's murder. They were here about the silliness with the courier in the hotel foyer.

He had almost made a gigantic gaffe.

One crisis had only passed when another sprang up. The garrulous drunk had caused the car park floodlights to be switched on. One spotlight just above the Vectra flooded over it. Every police officer in the country must be on the lookout for a maroon Vectra. Carver was relieved to see that the intensity of the surveillance light gave the Vectra a greenish colour, all except one spot on the car's bonnet that, by a cruel trick of light, had its maroon colour enhanced. Luckily for him the younger officer had to help his colleague to restrain the drunk, giving Carver the opportunity to move away from the Vectra. As quickly as the drunk had become confrontational, he now became compliant and quietly accompanied the older constable to the police car.

Now that the drunk had been arrested, would someone please switch off the floodlights.

'Now then, sir. About this incident in the hotel foyer this afternoon in which a Ms Esther Darby alleges that she was assaulted by you while she was delivering a package to hotel reception.'

'Assaulted?' said Carver with an air of jocular dismissiveness. 'Surely not, Constable.'

'Ms Darby felt quite threatened, sir.'

'A case of mistaken identity, Constable. I thought I knew her. She had gone past and, playing silly buggers, I grabbed Ms Darby by the arm.'

'Hotel security described your actions as,' he checked his notebook, '*over the top*, sir.'

'An exaggeration, I assure you. Realizing my mistake I immediately offered my profound apologies to the young lady. The foyer was crowded. Is it likely that, were my intentions of a malign nature, I would act in such a public place?'

The PC did not offer an opinion. 'In Brigham for pleasure or business, sir?'

'Business. But hopefully a bit of pleasure, too.'

'Staying long?'

'Returning home tomorrow evening.'

'And where would that be, sir? Home, I mean.'

Carver thought about lying, but he could not be sure whether the police had checked the hotel register.

'Loston.'

The officer's interest was immediate. 'Loston, eh? Been a nasty murder there.'

'Really?'

Carver felt the PC's intense scrutiny. 'A young woman. Found dead in her flat. A place called Cecil Street. Know of it?'

'Yes.'

'Close to where you live, is it, sir?'

'Not far.'

'Maybe you knew the young woman, then?'

'I doubt it.'

'Her name was Anne Tettle.'

Jack Carver made a pretence of thinking for a moment, and then lied. 'No.'

'Didn't have to come very far; that must be a blessing with roads clogged the way they are these days,' the constable said conversationally. 'Didn't have to leave too early, eh?'

'Not too early, no.'

'What time did you arrive, sir?'

'Around midday, I suppose.'

'Didn't see a hitch-hiker on the road, did you?'

Jack Carver's mouth was so suddenly dry that swallowing was difficult. 'No. Why?'

'A second murder. Cobley Wood. You'd have passed it.'

'Indeed.'

'Saw nothing at all, then?'

'No.'

'Look, sir, I'll have a word with Ms Darby,' he offered kindly. 'See what she has to say when I give her your explanation.'

'Very kind of you. Please give Ms Darby my sincerest apologies.'

'Meantime, if I could have some details, sir. Home address. Phone number. Mobile, if you have one.'

Carver lied. But he was careful to give a genuine Loston

area, and the Loston telephone code to prefix a false telephone number. His mobile number he pulled out of thin air.

'Well, sir, that's about it I reckon.' Jack Carver's heartbeat slowed a little. Then: 'Oh, do you own a car, sir?'

'Yes. If it were a dog it would bite you.' Jack Carver surprised himself with his acting skills.

The PC looked at the Renault Megane he was standing alongside – Larry Slater's Megane. He jotted down the car's registration number.

'Were you going somewhere just now, sir?'

'No. Some notes in the car I need.' Carver was acutely aware that the more lies he told, the greater would be the risk of tripping himself up.

The PC stepped aside to allow Carver access to the Megane. Forced to act, Carver made a show of searching his pockets before declaring, frustratedly, 'Damn, I've forgotten my keys. Changed my clothes.' To his ears, he sounded completely false.

'Happens all the time, sir. Changing from uniform to civvies and back to uniform. Best be off.'

Carver waited until the officers had driven away before hurrying to the Vectra. He had had a fortunate break, and he was not going to risk another encounter with the police. There had been no good reason that he could see why the officer would have asked him about his time of arrival other than to estimate by his average speed and distance covered where he might have been at the time Brenda Collins was murdered. Arriving at around midday, it would mean that he had left Loston after 11 a.m. instead of much earlier, a departure time which would rule him out of being on the road at the same time as Brenda Collins had been. But, of course, that would not hold water for very long. A check at the Coach and Four pub would quickly show that he had lied. And once the police discovered that he had told one lie, it would not take them long to find out that he had told several porkies. And they would soon learn that he had taken the best part of three hours to make the short journey from Loston to Brigham. Oh, yes. The police would be back, and soon.

'Not slapped in irons yet, Jack?'

Carver came up short.

'Not yet, Larry,' he returned cheerily.

'Complained did she? The woman you manhandled.'

'Manhandled? That's a bit dramatic, isn't it.'

'All sorted now, is it?'

'Nothing to sort, really.'

'Coming back inside?' Slater asked.

'Must just get some notes from the car.'

'Notes? Where's the old fly-by-the-seat-of-his-pants Jack Carver got to?'

Carver pretended to fumble around in the Vectra until Slater tired of waiting and went back inside. Once out of the car park, he relaxed a little. But his relief was short lived when the petrol indicator flashed. His mind shot back to the petrol station near Cobley Wood where the pumps had been out of order. He had forgotten to fill up later.

The engine dipped.

The traffic lights at a junction ahead changed to red.

CHAPTER TWELVE

DI Sally Speckle flung herself into the chair behind her desk, despondent. 'We're getting nowhere, are we, Andy. All we've got is a lot of ifs and maybes.'

Andy Lukeson understood and was sympathetic to Sally Speckle's need to make quick progress. It was her first murder, and all eyes were on her. And, regrettably, a lot of people would be waiting for her to fail. The failure, if failure there was, would, of course, be collective. But that was not the way things worked. The entire blame would rest squarely on the shoulders of the senior investigating officer. The police were no different from any other organization when it came to failure; someone would have to carry the can, be the scapegoat. And that someone would most definitely be DI Sally Speckle. She would, of course, remain a DI (no one of senior rank would want to admit to having got it wrong by demoting her), however, she would serve out her time for as long as she could take the humiliation, far removed from any investigation of importance, and certainly no way near a headline-grabbing double murder. Instead of eating continuous humble pie she would in all probability quit the force and there would be an ocean of relief that an embarrassing problem had been got rid of. In Andy Lukeson's experience, not many organizations were as unforgiving of failure as the police. And the pity would be that, in his opinion, the force would have lost a very good copper in Sally Speckle.

'Early days yet,' he offered his superior by way of consolation. 'Look on the bright side. We've got four suspects. The man who picked up Brenda Collins. Chambers and Burke. And Alfred Cannon, who has a history of violence and a very dodgy alibi, provided by a former cellmate.'

'A couple of convictions for soccer hooliganism a long time ago, Andy.'

'Soccer hooliganism is still violence.'

'But soccer hooliganism was and is a lot about people getting caught up in the fervour on the day. I'm sure that most soccer hooligans went on to be perfectly good citizens.'

'And some went on to become criminals like Cannon,' the DS pointed out. 'He's a burglar who might have mistimed.'

'Living in the Cecil Street house, would he risk thieving so close to home? And had Anne Tettle anything really worth stealing?'

'He could have known she had a laptop. Ready cash, if you know where to off-load it.'

'But Cannon would have known Tettle's routine. So if he was going to burgle her flat he'd not be caught napping, would he?'

'There's always the unexpected. Tettle could have popped out of the blue.'

'Cannon has no history of violent burglary,' Speckle pointed out.

'That we know of.'

'We have Cannon's prints and DNA on file. If he had been involved in violence after his soccer hooligan days, all of twenty years ago, it would surely have come to light. And there's not a sign so far of him having ever been in Tettle's flat, Andy.'

'Cannon is a pro, Sally. He'd be forensically aware. He'd have been in and out of Tettle's flat like the proverbial ghost.'

'OK. Granted. But where does Cannon fit in with Collins?'

'There, I'm stumped,' Lukeson conceded.

'That leaves us with the man from the pub and Chambers and Burke. Burke's and Chambers' fingerprints were in Tettle's flat but they both admit to having been there, so how useful is that as evidence? I don't imagine a QC would have any difficulty in persuading a jury as to its doubtful nature.'

'In Chambers' case, her being a friend of Tettle's, it's explainable. But Simon Burke's prints are another matter. He was not a friend, so therefore what was the purpose of his visit? And he was reluctant to be fingerprinted. He was not too keen either to give a DNA sample—'

'Neither was Alice Chambers. But, honestly, how many people are? It could be just simple apprehension on their part. There's something about being asked for a DNA sample that, by common perception, implies guilt. No smoke without fire and all of that.

'The lab is taking an age to come back with anything positive. Why can't it be like on TV?' Speckle sighed. 'A single hair found and five minutes later the lab analysis instantly pin-points the killer. Telly should be more bloody realistic, Andy. And not give everyone the idea that conclusive DNA results and a host of other things can be clutched out of thin air,' she clicked her fingers, 'just like so. Don't the public realize that in real life everything can't be neatly wrapped up before the next bloody commercial break! Jen Roberts, the tall woman who might be our murderer?' Speckle sighed.

Andy Lukeson raised a quizzical eyebrow. 'Motive?'

'Oh, shit. I'm clutching at straws, aren't I, Andy?'

'Clutch away,' Andy Lukeson encouraged. 'You just might clutch the right straw.'

'Roberts says she's not gay. But what if she's still in the closet, Andy? And had been nurturing a passion for Anne Tettle; a passion that got out of control?'

'Possible.'

'You don't sound convinced.'

He shrugged. 'Maybe there's a more mundane explanation.'

'Such as?'

'Some festering dispute from the hospice? Something in the past? Maybe they knew each other before? Or maybe instead of Roberts being gay, Tettle tried it on and found out that she wasn't?'

During training, there had been many examples of cases that had lost their way in the opening stages – those vital first hours and days, and had either been solved much later than they should have been with a lot more grief than there need have been, or had become cold cases – copper jargon for unsolved cases. All it took was one wrong conclusion and the investigation could be off the rails for a long time. Sally Speckle thought about the possibility she had been dreading since she had been promoted – the worst of all outcomes for any copper – the career-ending transfer of the investigation to another officer.

The result of the Tettle post mortem had confirmed what Alec Balson had predicted it would be, a straightforward smash and bash affair. The Collins post mortem had not yet been officially completed, but there was little doubt that the conclusion would be the same. In both murders, the pathologist had confirmed that indeed a hammer had been the murder weapon. At least that was one definite in a sea of possibles, and it was a link between the murders. Unless, of course, there were two killers with the same MO. And how likely was that?

Sid Fields, the forensic pathologist, had concurred with Alec Balson's opinion that the blows delivered to Tettle, considering the multiplicity and the variable degree of force used, might not have been inflicted by a naturally left-handed person. So were they looking for a right-handed killer, who had been forced to improvise rather than risk a fight back by Anne Tettle, as Alec Balson had speculated? Or (taking into account the Collins murder, which no one had any doubt had been the handiwork of a right-handed killer), was the killer trying actively to convey the impression that there were two killers? But if that were so, wouldn't such a cunning murderer have changed his or her MO in the Collins murder? It was highly improbable, were it the killer's intention to put the idea of two killers abroad, that he or she would murder both victims in exactly the same fashion.

Fields had opined that, under normal circumstances, if a woman was the killer she would, taking into account Tettle's height and the angle of the blows delivered, be approximately five foot eight inches tall. All legs and Twiggy thin. Roberts would fit the bill. However, Alice Chambers was petite, so that would rule her out as Tettle's murderer. Or would it? Because Fields had also advised that 'if the victim were crouching, demonstrating he raised his arms to ward off imaginary blows, 'it could significantly alter matters.' Alternatively, 'If the killer was above the victim, standing on something, that would also alter matters.'

And where did all that leave Simon Burke and the man who had picked up Collins? Burke, at a guess, was about six feet tall, but he might be an inch or two over or under. The man from the Coach and Four pub was described as being about the same height. Did Sid Fields assessment rule them in or out?

The pathologist would not commit himself.

'There are so many factors which might have come into

play, an inch or two might make all the difference or little at all,' had been his opinion.

And what about Collins's murder. She was about the same height as Tettle, give or take.

'Could it be the same killer?' Lukeson had asked.

The pathologist had considered the question before answering. 'Possible,' he had concluded. Which was not much help.

Circles within circles. Nothing strange in that. Andy Lukeson was on his seventh murder inquiry and all, with the exception of one, had been the same. And he knew that despite the marvels of forensic science, any investigating officer still, in most instances, needed a great dollop of luck to separate the circles.

Brenda Collins had now been positively identified by a friend with whom she had over-nighted in Loston, who had seen her E-FIT on the news. The woman had sworn that Collins had not been gay. But then the woman had also not known that Brenda Collins was on the game. So how well had she known Collins to begin with?

DC Helen Rochester entered the room.

'The search of Burke's house has turned up a pair of panties hidden in one of his shoes. A search of Tettle's flat turned up two pairs that matched that pair in a pack. We also have discs of pornography that he had downloaded, some of it sick and violent. A good deal of it to do with lesbians. There was also the remains of a recent fire in an out of the way part of his garden, behind some old sheds. The ashes have gone to the lab for analysis. He's waiting in interview room four.'

Had the luck which Andy Lukeson reckoned they would need, arrived?

'Let's go and hear what Burke has to say, Andy, shall we?' Speckle said, leaving her office with a new spring in her step.

Simon Burke looked sullen and angry. 'What game do you think you're playing at?' he challenged Speckle the second she entered the room. 'Your antics have ended my marriage, you do realize that, don't you?'

Speckle gave no quarter.

'If your marriage is finished, you finished it, Mr Burke.' A PC entered the interview room and whispered to Speckle. 'Show Mr Crookshaw in, Constable.'

'Thought I'd better have my solicitor present,' Burke said.

'It's your right,' Speckle said. She waited until Crookshaw had settled in before she continued: 'An item of clothing was found at your home, Mr Burke. This to be precise.' She held up an evidence bag containing a pair of panties. 'We believe it to be Ms Tettle's underwear.'

Burke looked in desperation at Crookshaw, who conversed with him briefly. Then Burke confirmed, 'Yes, it is.'

'How did you come by it?'

Burke mumbled, 'Stole it.'

'When?'

'When I was in her flat. I went to the loo and it was on the bathroom floor.'

'Why did you take it?'

He shrugged. 'I don't really know. One of those stupid spur of the moment things.'

'Are you sure the garment was on the bathroom floor, Mr Burke?' Simon Burke looked at Andy Lukeson. 'Or might you have removed it from Anne Tettle's person during an attempt at sexual intimacy?'

'Bloody hell!' Burke ranted. 'It was on the bathroom floor, I tell you.'

'Is there any evidence to suggest otherwise, Sergeant,' Crookshaw questioned, and added reprovingly in the absence of a reply from Lukeson, 'Let's have less of the creative thinking and stick to what is known, shall we.'

'Everything in Ms Tettle's flat was extremely clean, neat, tidy and well-ordered, Mr Crookshaw,' Lukeson said in defence of his line of questioning. 'It would be my opinion that Ms Tettle was not the kind of person who would discard her underwear on the bathroom floor.'

'You're opinion isn't worth a fig, Sergeant. It's what you can prove that counts.' Crookshaw looked to Speckle to rein in her sergeant. He was disappointed.

'Based on our observations, my sergeant's line of questioning is, I believe, valid, Mr Crookshaw,' Sally Speckle responded. 'Why was it necessary to use the toilet in Ms Tettle's flat, Mr Burke? Why not just pop across the landing to Ms Chambers' flat?'

Simon Burke shrugged. 'I don't know. Seems sensible now in hindsight.'

'Might it be that you intended to stay longer than Ms Tettle would have wished? That you didn't want to risk leaving, fearful that she would not welcome your return, perhaps?'

'No. You're completely twisting this whole thing,' Burke protested vehemently. 'Look, I had a drink, at Anne Tettle's invitation,' he stressed. 'Chatted for five or ten minutes and left.'

'But not empty handed,' said Lukeson, deadpan. 'Five or ten minutes. A very short period of time in which you found it necessary to use the loo, wouldn't you say? During the search of your home a number of pornographic discs were found—'

'Perfectly legal. Nothing to do with children.'

'—A number of which contained sadistic and violent material, some of this aimed at lesbians. Like that kind of thing, do you, Mr Burke?'

'Like it or not, Sergeant,' Crookshaw said. 'My client is guilty of nothing illegal.'

'I didn't say he was, Mr Crookshaw. I merely raised the content of these discs, particularly those dealing with lesbian scenes as a possible indicator of your client's . . . shall we say, *preferences*.'

'Really, Inspector,' Burke's solicitor blustered. 'I like Westerns, so does that indicate a secret longing to be a cowboy?'

Again, he got no leeway from Sally Speckle.

'The remains of a recent fire was found in your garden, Mr Burke,' she said. 'What did you burn?'

'Just some old magazines and newspapers.'

'What kind of magazines?'

'Just magazines. To do with antiques mostly.'

'Nothing you'd want to be rid of before the police arrived to search your house?'

'I hadn't expected the police to search my house, Inspector.'

'But you must have had an idea that they might,' Speckle said.

'If that were so, then why would I keep those discs to be found?'

'Simply because you hadn't time to dispose of them?'

'Do you intend to charge my client?' Crookshaw enquired of Sally Speckle. 'And if you do, what with?'

'Not at present, Mr Crookshaw. You're free to leave for now, Mr Burke.'

Pausing before he left, Burke stated, 'I didn't murder Anne Tettle, you know.'

'But did you murder Brenda Collins?' said Speckle, when he had left.

As she and Lukeson came from the interview room, a PC came to meet them. 'Harry Brown says that there's a lady to see you, ma'am. Says that it's in connection with the Tettle murder.'

A minute later, Speckle was in the reception area. Harry Brown, the desk sergeant, nodded in the direction of an elderly woman who was muttering to herself incoherently. 'I wouldn't get too excited,' he said. And on seeing what appeared to be a senile old woman, Sally Speckle agreed.

'You wanted to see me?'

The woman looked annoyed at the interruption to her conversation with some imaginary person. 'Do I?' she enquired brusquely.

'Yes.' Speckle glanced towards the desk sergeant who cast his eyes to heaven. 'You wanted to see me about the

Tettle murder. I'm DI Sally Speckle, the officer in charge of the investigation.'

'A female detective inspector,' the woman exclaimed. 'Times are indeed changing. And, no doubt, for the better.'

'Thank you. But female detective inspectors are not that uncommon any more.'

'Henry ... Henry ... Henry ...' the woman fretted. 'A type of house, you know.'

'I beg your pardon.'

'A house that Henry would have had.' The woman dived into a canvas bag that was big enough to hide a battleship in and came up with a magazine, opened at a partly completed crossword puzzle. 'Ten down, five letters,' she said, pointing.

'Tudor,' Speckle suggested.

The woman's intelligent blue eyes lit up. 'Of course! How silly of me. Henry the Eighth – Henry Tudor. The house of Tudor!' She looked with a new interest at Sally Speckle. 'You're the bright one, aren't you, m'dear.'

'A shot in the dark really.'

'Oh, don't be modest. I detest modesty. So wishy-washy, modesty. Do crosswords, do you, Inspector?'

'When I have the time, which isn't very often.'

The elderly woman tapped her forehead. 'Keeps the box of tricks ticking over, you know – crosswords. That and sex.' On seeing Speckle's astonishment, the woman laughed mischievously. 'If I could manage the latter, I dare say I wouldn't be so keen on the former, eh? The name's Henrietta Brewster – Miss,' she emphasized, seeming quite proud of her spinsterhood. Speckle took the bony hand

Miss Brewster proffered. It was cold to the touch, like elderly people's hands tend to be, and a chill went through her. The woman stuffed the magazine back into the tent-sized canvas bag and looked with unblinking concentration at Sally Speckle. Nothing so far had prepared the DI for what Henrietta Brewster said next:

'Now, then, Inspector. About Anne Tettle's murder. I know who did it.'

Just when he thought his luck had run out, Jack Carver found a garage. He filled up, conscious all the while of the forecourt CCTV. Was the cashier taking too much interest in him? Might she have seen the earlier newscast about the Cobley Wood murder in which his description and the Vectra's had been given.

'Going far?' the cashier enquired when he went to pay, though she did not seem to be a friendly type.

'Almost home,' Carver answered, as casually conversational as he could manage to be.

As he drove away the cashier's interest in him remained steadfast. He resisted the temptation to drive above the speed limit, and the suburbs of Brigham seemed to take an age to reach. But eventually, driving along a quiet road and reckoning that the risk of a chance encounter with the police was remote, Carver increased his speed, anxious to be clear of Brigham. And that was when the woman, dressed in dark clothes, her face ghostly in the Vectra's headlights, loomed up in front of him.

Carver swerved.

*

'You know the identity of Anne Tettle's killer?' Speckle checked, stunned.

'Unsavoury type,' said Henrietta Brewster, contemptuously. 'Saw him a couple of weeks ago in Anne's flat. Didn't like the look of him one little bit. Nice young woman, Anne. Always made time to stop and chat. The supermarket, that's where we first met. Got a bargain in fresh carrots, love carrots. My basket was rather heavy and Anne came to my assistance. Not many young people have time for an old fogey like me nowadays.'

'You saw this man in Anne Tettle's flat, you say, Miss Brewster? Do you mean that you met him there?'

'Oh, no.' Miss Brewster dived into the canvas bag again, and this time came up with a pair of binoculars. 'Saw him through these. They're very good. The army uses the same kind, you know. Bought them from one of those catalogues.' She put the binoculars to her eyes. 'I might as well have been right there in the room, you know.'

Speckle again exchanged glances with Harry Brown, his scepticism now replaced by curiosity. Sally Speckle was sure that the desk sergeant was trying to imagine, as she was, Henrietta Brewster as a peeping Tom.

'I use these to look at the river from my attic window. I live one street away from Cecil Street on Oak Drive. A three-storey monstrosity that's quite impractical nowadays with the cost of upkeep. But it's been the family home for over a hundred years, and one must do one's best to hold on, don't you think, Inspector?'

'Of course, Miss Brewster. One must.'

'From the attic I can see out over the smaller houses in

Cecil Street to the river, you see. Oh, dear me. I'm rambling on, aren't I?'

Sally Speckle smiled indulgently.

'Do you like birds, Inspector?'

'Yes. But I really don't know much about them, Miss Brewster.'

'One can see some quite interesting birds on the river, you know. I know all their routines and habits by now,' Henrietta Brewster boasted proudly. 'Used to go down to the river to sketch the birds, but that's impossible now. Lots of dodgy types hanging around.'

Dodgy. It was a word that was completely at odds with the very proper Henrietta Brewster.

'Times have changed,' Speckle sympathized.

Warming to her subject, Miss Brewster said, with an air of shocked incomprehension, 'Only last evening I saw a jogger dump a hold-all in the river. She just threw it in as she ran past. Quite a disgraceful carry on! Don't these people understand that the river is home to these beautiful and elegant creatures?'

'You're a birdwatcher, then?'

Henrietta Brewster looked enquiringly at Sally Speckle, and then laughed heartily. 'You thought that I was a peeping Tom, didn't you, Inspector?' Sally Speckle glared at Harry Brown as he put his hand over his mouth and turned away. 'As, obviously, did your sergeant.' Now it was the DI's turn to be smug. 'Oh, never you mind, m'dear. I can see how you might think that.

'Anyway, I saw this man in Anne Tettle's flat, arguing with her. His attitude was quite threatening. I thought about phoning the police, but I feared that Anne would be displeased and' – her gaze went from Speckle to Brown – 'like you two, she might get the wrong end of the stick and think that I was spying on her, when all I was doing was watching a kingfisher swooping down and her window came into view quite by accident.'

'About what time last evening was this, Miss Brewster?'

'Oh, not last evening, m'dear. Must be a fortnight ago.' Sally Speckle's disappointment was evident. 'Oh, I see, you thought that it was last evening I witnessed this argument. No, no. Last evening was when I saw him leave the house.'

Sally Speckle's heart did a little jig.

'The same man you saw arguing with Ms Tettle?' she checked.

'Oh, definitely.' Miss Brewster became thoughtful. 'At least I supposed he was leaving the house.'

'You supposed?'

'Well, I actually saw him on the steps outside the house and I naturally assumed that he had been inside and was leaving.' She frowned worriedly. 'But perhaps he'd never got in.'

'What time was this, Miss Brewster?'

'Six thirty.'

'You're very positive.'

'Well, my sister phoned at a quarter past six. We spoke for about ten minutes, then I went back upstairs to the attic to resume my birdwatching. So, give five minutes for that, which would make it half past six, give or take a minute.'

Speckle could hardly contain her excitement. Half past six was within the time frame during which Anne Tettle had been murdered.

'Can you describe this man, Ms Brewster?'

'Dark hair, going grey, receding at the temples. Pale. Weak sort of face. Ears on the large side.'

Speckle was astonished.

'You've a very good eye for detail,' she complimented the elderly woman.

'About five foot ten,' Miss Brewster continued, accepting the compliment in her stride. 'Would be six feet, maybe a touch over it, if he hadn't had rounded shoulders – layabout shoulders, I'd call them. Lazy lot, I shouldn't wonder. Late thirties to early forties.'

Based on Sid Fields estimation of Tettle's killer's height, the difference between five feet ten inches and six feet, made the man's height very interesting. The man who had picked up Brenda Collins had dark hair, going grey. His age had been put at early forties. However, Fred Clampton, the elderly man who had watched the man leave the pub with Collins, had said that the man had strong features. But then the barmaid had described him as sly-looking. The man's E-FIT, though pretty much a hotch-potch of competing features, might still prove very interesting.

Henrietta Brewster stood up. 'Hope you find this thug, Inspector.'

'I'm sure we shall,' Speckle said confidently. 'You've been most helpful. Before you go, I wonder if you'd look at a picture of a suspect?'

'An E-FIT thingy?'

'Yes. You're very knowledgeable.'

'I devour police series on the telly,' Ms Brewster said, as

if she were confessing a grievous sin.

'Yes, they can be quite informative,' said Sally Speckle. 'If, at times, a bit off the mark.'

'Boring if they had every little thing right,' Brewster opined. 'Dramatic licence and all that, you know.'

A short time later, holding her breath, Speckle showed Henrietta Brewster an E-FIT of the man who had left the Coach and Four pub with Brenda Collins. The elderly woman's response was immediate and very definite.

'Not him.'

'You're sure?'

'Positive, m'dear.' Once more she dived into the canvas bag. 'That's the man,' she said, handing over a detailed drawing of the man she had seen; a drawing that leapt off the page with detail. Speckle recalled that Miss Brewster had mentioned going down to the river to sketch. 'Went to art college.' Her gaze reached back to the distant past. 'Wanted to be an artist more than anything else. But my mother, who could be quite a tyrant, thought that being an artist was not a respectable career for a young lady.

'I joined the Civil Service to please her, with the intention of one day taking up the brush. But mother lived to be eighty-six, still every bit as fixed in her views. And I, at fifty-two, was still every inch in dread of her, as I had been as a youngster.'

Miss Brewster sighed wearily.

'A coward to the last, I'm afraid, Inspector.' She tapped the drawing. 'Looks a bad lot, doesn't he? Hate men with weak chins. Sorry I didn't get round earlier, m'dear. Ate

123

something that disagreed with me. Laid me low for a while.'

'Hope you're fully recovered?'

'At my age it's always a case of being as best as one can be, Inspector.'

'I'm glad you did come round, Miss Brewster. Now, shall I get someone to run you home?'

Henrietta Brewster's intelligent blue eyes lit up. 'In a squad car?'

'What else?'

'I shall enjoy that,' Henrietta Brewster enthused.

Jack Carver's plans to quit Brigham went up in smoke. The Vectra veered across the road, side-swiped an oncoming vehicle and went headlong into a garden wall which, to judge by the catastrophic impact, had been built like the Great Wall of China. The front of the Vectra crumpled. There was a waft of hot oil, accompanied by a plume of thick, black smoke.

The engine coughed and died.

'Phone the police, Charlie,' screamed the female passenger of the vehicle he had collided with, thrusting a mobile phone at the driver.

The driver of the vehicle looked murderous as he examined the long tear on the side of the Honda four-wheel-drive. Carver looked about for the woman who had caused the accident, but she had used the confusion of the collision to vanish. People were coming from houses. Passers-by were stopping. With the road blocked, other traffic was piling up. In minutes the police would arrive. Jack Carver decided that there was only one thing to do.

Leg it.

CHAPTER THIRTEEN

Not wanting to be alone, Mel Carver went next door to her neighbour Jen Roberts. 'Just returning this,' she said, handing over an old photograph album as an excuse. The album had belonged to Arthur Granger, the man whom Roberts had been visiting at the hospice and who had died a couple of weeks previously. Jen had lent Mel the album to look through, and Mel had not wanted to upset her by telling her that she had no interest.

'Oh, you shouldn't have bothered, Mel. That would have waited.'

'I've had it for ages, Jen.'

'Did you enjoy looking at the photographs?'

'Yes, I did,' Mel lied. 'Arthur Granger was quite a snapper, wasn't he?'

'Drink? A nip of brandy, maybe?' Jen Roberts suggested.

'Lovely.'

'A very interesting man, Arthur Granger,' Roberts said, handing Mel her drink. 'Used to work in the Saudi oil industry. Right or wrong, he blamed that for his lung cancer, ignoring his sixty-a-day habit. Of course that was long before terrorists started kidnapping and murdering people just because they were Brits.' Roberts placed the album on a coffee table and opened it. She selected a group photograph and pointed to a very distinguished-looking man. 'That's Arthur Granger. Quite impressive, don't you think?'

'Very,' Mel agreed. 'They look happy.' Mel pointed to a man and a woman. The man was hugging the woman to him. She was smiling adoringly up at the bearded man. 'Head over heels in love, I'd say.'

Jen Roberts studied the woman. 'You can see the love shining in her eyes, can't you?'

'Wonder where they are now?' Mel pondered. 'If they married? What happened to them? Whenever I look at old photographs, I can't help wonder about the people in them.'

'No,' Jen Roberts said. 'They never married. They planned to marry a couple of months after that picture was taken, but the man did a runner. Left the woman holding the baby, literally.

'Bastard!'

'That's men for you, Mel. Broken-hearted and despairing, the woman hanged herself.'

'How horrible.'

Jen Roberts sprang out of her chair. 'Another drink?'

'No, thanks. It's late. I'd best be off.'

'Yes, sir.' Speaking on the phone, DI Sally Speckle rolled her eyes. 'Yes, I can understand that the press will be baying, sir.' DS Andy Lukeson could hear Sermon Doyle's booming voice over the phone. 'Yes, I understand, sir. . . . Of course, we'll pull out all the stops, of that you can be sure. . . . Of course, sir. Fully informed.'

She replaced the phone.

DC Helen Rochester placed the cup of sweet tea that she had got from the canteen for Andy Lukeson on the desk, near the drawing of the man Henrietta Brewster had seen arguing with Tettle in her flat, and whom she had seen the previous evening outside Tettle's flat.

'Sermon giving us grief, then?'

Sally Speckle was not sure if she approved of her sergeant's mode of address for a senior officer. 'Yes, that was Chief Superintendent Doyle,' she said pointedly. But the fact was that anyone out of earshot of the Chief Super used his nickname. And she suspected that he knew they did. In fact she was certain that Doyle missed very little of what went on.

'Sure you wouldn't like a cuppa, ma'am?' Rochester enquired of her DI.

A timely, welcome and diplomatic change of subject matter, Lukeson thought.

'No, thanks. Frankly, tea right now would be a poor substitute for a brandy.'

'I know him,' Rochester said, picking up Henrietta Brewster's drawing from Speckle's desk. The statement had Speckle and Lukeson sitting up. 'He was involved in a dust-up at the opening of the new branch of the New World Building Society a couple of weeks ago. Bob Waters and I were passing in a squaddie at the time. This bloke was having a right go about having had his apartment repossessed.'

'So who is he?' Speckle asked.

'Didn't get his name?'

'So he wasn't detained?' Lukeson groaned.

'No.'

'Why not?'

'There was a building society bigwig, ah . . . Roycroft – Julius Roycroft. Didn't want any of it. But if they repossessed his gaff, they'll have an address for him.'

'They'll have the address of the apartment they repossessed,' Speckle said. 'And someone there might know where he's got to. And if our luck is in, the building society might have communicated with him at his current address.'

'There was a woman there, too. On a right rant about her sister having got the sack. Threatening all sorts of nasties.'

'Some opening,' Lukeson commented.

'Was she with this man?' Speckle asked.

'Hard to say. They were both having a go, but maybe it was an impromptu alliance. It was all a bit hectic.'

'Did you get the woman's name?' the DI enquired hopefully.

'No. This bloke Roycroft just wanted them moved on.' She chuckled. 'The man on the receiving end of this aggro said that he wished he was off playing golf.'

'Golf?' Speckle said. 'Check with Loston golf club, Helen. If this man is a member, they'll have a home address for him, I shouldn't wonder.'

Rochester picked up the nearest phone.

'No,' Speckle said. 'I think the personal touch will get better results.'

Helen Rochester departed to do as she was bid.

'Like a break from it all, Andy? A quick visit to the Plodders Well?' The invitation surprised Lukeson. They had only been a partnership for a very short time and were more or less still getting use to each other, and from what he had learned, or thought he had, he would have expected Sally Speckle to adhere strictly to the formalities of rank. Of course other DIs and their sergeants shared a social as a well as a working life, but only after a long time during which the structures of rank became blurred. 'Maybe it's not such a good idea,' she said, interpreting Andy Lukeson's silence as a rejection of her invitation.

'I'd love to,' he said.

Jack Carver sprang into a shop doorway as a police car sped past. He thanked the vandals who had smashed the street light directly above. As he stepped back out of the doorway it began to rain again. Where could he go? By now the police would have got his name and address from his car registration and, as he'd paid with cash for petrol, that left him with only his credit card. He dared not use that to pay for accommodation for fear of the transaction being traced. There was nothing he could do but try and find somewhere to doss down, and hope that by morning he would have thought of a way to get safely out of Brigham.

The Plodders Well (officially known as the King's Head),

was so called because it was the favourite haunt of off-duty police officers, or those taking a short break (their superiors would hope) as DI Sally Speckle and DS Andy Lukeson were.

Though every copper who passed through the doors of the Plodders Well came determined not to bring with him or her the case they were currently working on, inevitably that was what happened. Sally Speckle was no exception.

'Bludgeoning is messy, Andy. The murderer couldn't avoid being splattered. So he just couldn't walk away. It would mean that the killer would have to take a big risk, even leaving the house and getting into a car. Cecil Street is a quiet residential street. It's pretty dead after the main rush home in the evening. Also, at any second a door within the house could have opened as he went past.'

'The killer could simply have changed clothes,' Lukeson said. 'Like Alice Chambers did when she wanted to shed her wet clothes after going to meet her chatroom date.'

'Clever, that,' Speckle said. 'The killer would need something to put the bloodstained clothing in, a hold-all or a rucksack. Something that would zip up. He couldn't risk a plastic bag.'

'And if he was foolish, the killer might have held on to whatever he carried the clothes in.'

'That would be a bloody stupid thing to do, Andy.'

'Ever hear of Sylvia Murray?'

'Before my time.'

'Staged a burglary then smashed her husband's skull, to take advantage of a spate of local burglaries to hide her crime. Might have got away with it, had she not been reluctant to part with the murder weapon, a Waterford crystal decanter. Too valuable to throw away, she said. In Sylvia Murray's case, meanness was her undoing.'

'Nothing turned up in the search of Chambers' flat. What do you make of what we found in Burke's house? That stuff on the discs was warped.'

'If every porn downloader was a murderer we wouldn't have enough gaols to hold them all.'

'Maybe Burke has made the leap from watching to acting out?' Speckle said. 'He wouldn't be the first. And his little peculiarity. What do you make of that?'

'Not much. Again if every panties fancier became a killer . . .' Lukeson shrugged.

'But sometimes a person with Burke's range of pleasures does become a killer. Maybe something will turn up in the ashes from the fire in his garden.'

'I'm not holding my breath,' Lukeson responded. 'Like I said, I think Burke is a tosser. But I wouldn't deny his intelligence. I simply can't see him burning bloodstained clothes in his back garden.'

'Maybe he thinks he's too clever for a couple of plodders like us. A lot of murderers have very big egos.'

'Andy!' Lukeson turned to face a cherub-faced man, Detective Constable Larry Aiken from Fraud, bearing down on him. 'You've won the station monthly, my son.' The station monthly, which Larry Aiken referred to, was a monthly draw which the station personnel had begun as a Christmas fund a couple of years previously, and had continued on throughout the year ever since. Aiken cupped an ear. 'What's that, Andy? Drinks are on you?' A rousing cheer raised the rafters of the Plodders Well. The hundred quid, as was the norm, vanished across the bar. Somehow, the winner was always told of his good fortune in the Plodders Well.

'Somehow, I can't quite see Alice Chambers as the killer,' said Sally Speckle, as the cheering died down. 'Blunt instruments aren't a woman's thing, are they. A nice bit of poison is more a woman's way. Or is that very Victorian?'

Speckle's mobile rang.

'Speckle. Great!' she exclaimed excitedly. 'I'll be along right away. They've found a computer diary on Tettle's laptop,' she told Lukeson.

Huddled in an alley doorway with the rain driving in on him, Jack Carver's hope of evading the police slid depressingly down the scale of probability. He was without a car. By now the bus and rail stations were probably being watched. He could try and hitch a lift (ironic that, he thought), but after Brenda Collins's murder no one would be too keen to pick up a hitcher. On the contrary, they would probably report a man hitching to the police. Maybe he should face reality and help the police with their enquiries, he thought. But, of course, any benefit which he might have had, had he done that at first, would now be most definitely negated by the fact that his belated willingness to come forward would simply be seen as him having run out of options.

6 August.
Good news from Mandy. The lump was benign. Another lousy day at work. Mrs Rodgers died. Sweet old dear.

HE phoned.
Told HIM to piss off and stop bothering me! Spoke to Sue
about going back to London. Not keen to have me around.
Must be bedding Ingrid in a frenzy.

7 August.
Stomach cramp. Dodgy pizza, I reckon. Work not too bad.
Gerrard the Hun away. Made enquiries about going to
Thailand on hols.

Sally Speckle scrolled ahead, anxious to find any more
references to HE. Hoping that HE would have a name.

12 Aug.
Told HIM that if he didn't stop making a nuisance of
himself, I'd go to the police.

'Motive,' Lukeson murmured.

What a price to pay for getting a couple of doors fixed.
Yipeee! Lost twelve pounds on new diet. Bum still too big. B
likes it though. Some consolation.

'B? Brenda?' Speckle wondered. She scrolled ahead
again, keeping a keen eye out for any further mention of
the mysterious man.

15 August.
Shit! HE is getting scary. What's his game? He knows I'm
not interested. Sue phoned. Terrible state. Ingrid upped and

left. Invited me to come and stay. Told her to shove it. Met
Jen Roberts on the riverwalk. Almost told her I fancied her.
Wonder what she'd have said? Told Jen she was daft if she
got involved again in Gerrard's adopt a patient lark. Might
go to the Twisted Finger after all.

'Twisted Finger? Isn't that the gay bar in Wellington
Square?'

'Yes,' Lukeson confirmed. 'Maybe Tettle befriended a
bad one after all.'

Crossed paths with Simon Burke, leering and touchy-feely
as usual. Creep! What does Alice see in him? Makes my skin
crawl. Right old fart! Doesn't understand the word no!

'Doesn't seem that Burke was ploughing fertile ground,'
Lukeson observed.

'That's it. The fifteenth is the last entry. Might Burke be
He, Andy?'

'So what happened in Anne Tettle's life between her last
diary entry and when she was murdered? Pity she lent the
laptop to Roberts. If she hadn't we might be able to go
straight to the killer's door.'

Sally Speckle rubbed tired eyes. 'I think that's enough for
today, don't you?'

'It has been pretty hectic,' Lukeson agreed.

'Why didn't Tettle name *HE*? Why didn't she just say
that blah blah was making a nuisance of himself?'

'*HE* is more mysterious? Maybe in an odd sort of way,
she was enjoying the attention.'

135

'From someone she described as scary?'

'Serial killers get hundreds of letters every week from women,' Lukeson pointed out. 'And they're bloody scary!'

'Better ask the phone companies for a list of calls made to Tettle's number, and from whom. Burke is an accountant. Hardly the kind to be fixing doors, as the man Tettle was talking about did.'

'This is the age of multi-skilling, Sally.'

'Let's start with the obvious. Phones registered to tradesmen. Handymen. And anyone with form for making a nuisance of themselves.'

'Sarge,' DC Helen Rochester came running along the hall after Lukeson. 'Sorry this took so long. The golf club got a bit stroppy.' Lukeson read the note Rochester handed him. The name of the manager of the Loston branch of the New World Building Society interested him, but not as much as where he lived – number eleven Allworth Avenue.

Right next door to Jen Roberts.

DI Sally Speckle was getting into her car, a Punto that had seen better days, when Andy Lukeson caught her up. 'I don't think it's quite time to call it a day yet,' he told her.

'Could I speak to Jack?' the man on the phone asked.

Police? Mel was immediately on guard. 'I'm sorry. Jack isn't here.'

'Are you Mrs Carver?' the caller enquired.

'Yes.' Mel thought she sounded breathless.

'My name is Frank Crowther.' Didn't the police usually give their rank? 'A blast from the past, you might say.'

Not the police then. Mel was relieved.

'Jack and I did a stint in Saudi,' Crowther explained. 'In the Financial Services game.'

'Jack never said.'

'Oh, it was a long time ago. I'm based in the Argentine now, still doing the same thing. Old Jack still sporting a beard, eh? I'm at the end of a business jaunt and thought that Jack might like a trip down memory lane.'

'I'm sure he'd have loved to. But I'm afraid he won't be back for a couple of days.'

'Oh, bugger! Next time round, maybe? Give him my best.'

'I will.'

' 'Bye.'

Mel Carver replaced the phone, her mood thoughtful. Something niggled annoyingly at the back of her mind.

CHAPTER FOURTEEN

DS Andy Lukeson turned into Allworth Avenue, a road of pre-war houses with the kind of gardens that present-day buyers could only dream about, and on which any half-baked property developer would erect ten town houses, developerspeak for slap-ups.

All the houses were of the same design, and yet managed to look individual and different. Allworth Avenue was of an era in which builders and craftsmen took pride in their work and believed in delivering good work for reasonable return. Craftsmanship was etched in every stone and timber, as evident in these properties as it was lacking in newer structures. 'None of your stud walls and postage-stamp gardens here,' Lukeson said appreciatively. Midway along the road he stopped. The Carver house was in darkness.

Going upstairs, from the landing window Jen Roberts saw Speckle and Lukeson get out of the car.

Mel Carver was startled by the sudden buzz of the doorbell. About to go upstairs, she turned round and knocked against the hall table. The empty flower vase on the table wobbled. Mel grabbed at the vase to steady it but it slid away from her grasp, destined to smash on the hall floor. She grabbed it just as it went over the edge. Luckily the house was in darkness (because since she had spoken to Jack she had had too much to ponder on and had put off the lights to discourage any visitors) and she had probably not been seen. The doorbell buzzed again. This time more urgently. Had the police (Mel instinctively knew the callers were police officers) seen the movement in the hall after all?

She backed into the kitchen and was almost caught in the beam of a torchlight shining through the kitchen window. Fortunately it was still bobbing about unfocused. She slid into an alcove near the kitchen door, pressing back against the wall as the beam of the torch swept past like a watchtower searchlight in an old B&W prisoner-of-war film, monitoring the barbed wire fence for escapes. The doorbell buzzed again.

Strident. Piercing. Accusing.

As the beam of light came back across the kitchen more slowly, probing the darkness with greater purpose, it edged up to where Mel was hiding. She tried to squeeze further into the alcove, but she was already flat against the wall. She pulled the raincoat she had hung there earlier across her, and immediately fretted that she might have made a mistake. The coat would cover to her knees. Would that only make her lower legs more obvious?

The beam of light reached the edge of the alcove and

stopped. Mel's ears were filled with the thunder of her heart. Surely, she thought, even if the police officer at the kitchen window had not seen her he must hear her heartbeat. She glanced down as the beam of light skimmed past the toecaps of her shoes, thankfully black. Relieved, she heard the crunch of footsteps on the gravel path at the side of the house. Mel Carver's breath came in great gasps as lungs, stretched to breaking point, sought relief. Her every instinct was to flee the kitchen immediately for the safety of upstairs. But she would have to be patient. She heard a car start up and drive off before she left the kitchen.

Mel was going upstairs when the doorbell buzzed again.

'Mrs Carver,' a woman called out. 'This is the police. We'd like a word, please.' She had been lulled into a false sense of security by the sound of the car's departure. One of the officers had driven off, while the other waited. Clever. 'Please open the door, Mrs Carver,' said the woman impatiently. Obviously the kitchen alcove had not hidden her as well as she thought it had.

Trapped, Mel had no choice.

Admitting the police officers, she now worried about the impression of guilt her attempted evasion must have made.

'Mrs Carver?' the female officer checked.

'Yes.'

'I'm Detective Inspector Sally Speckle. And' – she waited for Lukeson to arrive – 'this is Detective Sergeant Lukeson. It's actually your husband we have come to see, Mrs Carver.'

'Jack is not here.'

'Where might he be, then?'

'I don't know where he is,' Mel answered truthfully, because he had left the hotel in Brigham. Then, lying: 'Fishing trip.' She knew that it was silly to lie. It would not take the police long to find out that she had. But right now she had to get rid of them, to regain her composure, to get time to be able to think straight. 'Scotland. Waiting for him to phone,' she added, impulsively. Having some strange idea that her second lie made her first lie more believable.

'We were hoping to ask him about an incident at the opening of the new building society branch of which he's the manager. There was an incident with a protester. We have reason to believe that this man may be able to help us with certain enquiries we are presently making, Mrs Carver.'

Mel's relief was great. The police had not come about Jack at all. 'When he phones, I'll get Jack to contact you at once, Inspector.'

'If you would, please.'

'Where in Scotland would that be?' Lukeson enquired.

'Jack said he'd let me know when he got settled,' Mel said. 'Look, I'm sorry that I can't be of more help. But as soon as I hear from Jack—'

'Thank you, Mrs Carver.' Speckle handed Mel her card. 'He can contact me at this number. Jittery,' she observed on leaving. 'And why delay opening the door to us?'

'It's late. She wasn't to know we were the police.'

From the sitting-room window, Mel Carver watched as the police went next door to Jen Roberts.

'Inspector. Sergeant,' Roberts intoned in mock surprise.

'You're out and about late.'

'May we come inside?' Lukeson asked.

Roberts made no objection, and led them to the sitting-room where she indicated the sofa while she remained standing. Seated, Andy Lukeson became interested in the battered photo album on the coffee table, where Mel Carver had left it when she had returned it earlier. 'May I?' He picked up the album. 'Family history?'

'No, Sergeant. It's just an old album I got from a man I used to visit at the hospice. I told you about Arthur Granger, didn't I?'

'Yes.' Lukeson began his perusal at the page at which Mel had left the album open; the page with the group photograph she and Roberts had been discussing earlier. 'Hard hats and hot sun,' Lukeson observed. 'Middle East, at a guess.'

'Yes. Saudi Arabia,' Roberts said.

'They look a happy bunch. And why not? Lots of sun instead of dreary rain.'

To Sally Speckle's annoyance, Lukeson flicked the page. What was he up to?

'That's more familiar.' He turned the album to Roberts to show her a photograph of a bleak winter moor.'

'Yorkshire,' Roberts said. 'Where Arthur Granger came from. Lived right on the edge of the moor.'

'He must have welcomed Saudi Arabia after that.'

'Oh, I don't know. Moor for desert. Just two different kinds of bleakness, wouldn't you say?'

He flicked another page of the album. 'Did you know that Anne Tettle kept a computer diary, Ms Roberts?'

Just about to interrupt their trip down memory lane, Sally Speckle was glad she had not. Clever sod, Andy Lukeson. Relaxed, social chit-chat, then pop your question off-handedly. She had a lot to learn from her sergeant.

'No,' Roberts replied, unfazed. 'Though I'm not surprised. Anne was a computer buff.'

'In it, Ms Tettle makes reference to a man, but unfortunately she didn't identify him. She only referred to the man as *HE*. You have no idea who this man might be?'

'None. Odd. Anne of all people having a mystery male admirer.'

'Oh, he wasn't an admirer. Well, not in the best meaning of the word. Seemed to be making a nuisance of himself. Ms Tettle described him as scary.'

'Good grief!'

'In her diary she also makes a reference to you.'

'Really? Flattering, I hope?'

'Depends.'

'I'm intrigued, Sergeant. Depends on what?'

'On how you might perceive her comments.'

'What was it Anne said?'

'That she fancied you,' Lukeson stated bluntly.

Jen Roberts gave a little laugh. 'Why should that surprise you? Anne was gay, Sergeant. I suspect she fancied many women.'

Speckle took up the questioning.

'How might you have reacted, had she acted on her impulse, Ms Roberts?'

'I'd have probably laughed, Inspector.'

'You wouldn't have been angry?'

'Angry? No. Anne is, or rather was, what she was.'

'Well, would you have been pleased, then?'

'Completely neutral, I'd say.' Roberts shook her head. 'God, but you lot are still back in the Dark Ages, aren't you. Guilty by association is alive and well. I think I've had about enough for now.'

'Just a few more questions,' Lukeson said, trenchantly.

'Well, get on with it then,' Jen Roberts responded after a brief, tense stand-off.

'In her diary, Ms Tettle clearly links this man to someone who did some work for her. Apparently he repaired some doors.'

'Doors?'

'That seems to have struck a chord,' Lukeson observed. 'You know this man?'

'Yes. I sent him round to Anne. There has to be some mistake. Jack isn't like that.'

'Jack?'

'Jack Carver. My next-door neighbour. He's into DIY. He went round to fix Anne's doors when she was having difficulty in getting the landlord to live up to his maintenance obligations. But there has to be some mistake. Jack Carver is very far removed from being scary.'

On his way out, caught by a draught, the sitting-room door blew in and Lukeson reached out to put his hand against it to stop it striking the unaware Sally Speckle. Off balance, he bumped against a table, knocking off a photograph, the glass of which shattered. 'Sorry.' He picked up the picture frame. 'I'll get this seen to.'

'No need.'

144

'I'd prefer to, please.'

The photograph was of Jen Roberts, much younger but readily recognizable. She was with another woman, whom she was hugging.

'My sister, Sergeant,' Roberts said, stiffly. 'Before you put two and two together and get five.'

'Sorry, again. I'll get this back to you as soon as I can. Goodnight.'

Outside, Speckle said, 'Time for another chat with Mrs Carver, I reckon.'

DC Charlie Johnson listened to the information the telephone company was passing to him, writing down the names and addresses of callers to Anne Tettle's phone in the last couple of weeks. 'Say again?' he said, sitting up. He wrote down and underlined the name: Graham Williams, Flat 12, Olten Court.

CHAPTER FIFTEEN

Going upstairs behind Detective Constable Helen Rochester, PC Brian Scuttle cursed his luck that she was in a long-term relationship with a bloke in Traffic, otherwise he might very well have made a move on her. He might still do, he thought. All's fair in love and war and all that. They were at Olten Court, a foul-smelling block of flats that had traces, like the sweeping marble stairs, of a more elegant and posher past. Rochester stopped outside flat number twelve, the spanking new door of which was completely at odds with its grungy frame. The door even had a gleaming brass knocker, which DC Rochester chose in preference to a bell on which someone had stuck chewing-gum. The man who answered was the man whom Henrietta Brewster had drawn with remarkable detail, capturing the very dislikable essence of Graham Williams.

'What do you lot want?' Williams asked aggressively.

'Mr Graham Williams?' Helen Rochester checked.

'Lost, are ya, *dearie*?' He sneered.

'Confirm your name!' Scuttle barked.

'Yeah. I'm Graham Williams,' he responded truculently.

'And keep a civil tongue in your head,' Scuttle warned.

'Ooohhh!' Williams taunted Helen Rochester. 'Feel safe with a big, burger-devouring constable to protect ya?'

Scuttle moved threateningly towards Williams. Helen Rochester placed a restraining hand on his arm. Though she was chuffed by her colleague's old-fashioned chivalry, she was also annoyed that Scuttle should think that she could not handle a tearaway like Williams.

'Back on your leash, then,' Williams goaded the PC. 'Like a good little boy.' Suddenly and frighteningly, his anger flared. 'It's that cow, innit? She said she'd have me done.' He shook his head in wonder. 'Don't know why I wanted to get in the poxy cow's knickers to start with.'

He winked leerily at Scuttle. 'Any port in a storm, eh, Constable?'

'Mind if we come inside?' Rochester asked.

'And if I say no?'

'Then I'll ask you to accompany PC Scuttle and me to the station,' Rochester said resolutely. 'Why go to all that bother for a couple of minutes' inconvenience now?'

Grudgingly, Williams stepped aside, his look furious. 'Nothing really happened, you know. Don't know what the fuss is all about. Felt her tit, that's all.' DC Rochester reckoned that Graham Williams's anger was never far below the surface, and it was obvious that he did not hold women in high esteem. 'Linda White would let you screw her for a bag of crisps.' Williams gave Scuttle a man of the world wink. 'You know the kind, Constable. Knickers down in a flash. Linda White invented the quickie.'

He gave Helen Rochester a cheeky-chappy grin.

'No offence, ma'am,' he said in a GI accent, with a brisk salute.

'Do you know a woman by the name of Anne Tettle?' Rochester asked.

'Never heard of her.'

'Sure about that?' Scuttle pressed.

'Yeah. I'm sure. Anyway, what's this Tettle bitch got to do with Linda White?'

'Nothing,' Helen Rochester said.

'Then why did you let me rattle on about what happened down the pub?' Williams ranted.

'We didn't solicit any information on what happened down the pub,' the DC said. 'You volunteered the information.'

'Did the cow even complain?'

'No, Mr Williams. That I know of, Ms White has not made a complaint to the police.'

'I should have known. If that slag reported every time a bloke tried it on, you lot would be writing 'til Doomsday!'

'Have you been in Cecil Street recently, Mr Williams?'

'Cecil Street? Where's that?'

'How long have you lived in Loston?' Scuttle asked.

'A coupla years.'

'And you don't know where Cecil Street is? Pull the other one, mate!'

Williams became even shiftier than was normal. 'Look, it was only a fiver. It was sitting there, asking to be nicked.'

'Where in Cecil Street was this?'

'One of them big old houses with twenty flats in it.'

'Did it have a number?'

'Six, I think.'

'When were you there?' Rochester asked.

'A coupla weeks ago. I went there to quote for a job. Not that it was much of a job. Just some sagging doors to fix.'

Aware of the references in Anne Tettle's computer diary to a mysterious man who had fixed doors for her, Helen Rochester's interest in Graham Williams sharpened.

'Did you get the job?'

'No. Said she'd phone. Never did. Pure waste of my time, it was,' he grumbled.

'Not completely. You nicked a fiver,' Scuttle reminded him.

'Was the woman's name Anne Tettle?' Rochester questioned.

He shrugged. 'There was a letter on the table next to the fiver addressed to Anne Tettle. So I suppose she was this bitch Tettle.'

Rochester's mobile rang.

'So why did you deny knowing her?' Scuttle demanded to know.

'You're not exactly the force's brightest wick, are you, mate?' Williams said, exasperated. 'I nicked from her, didn't I?'

'How did Ms Tettle know of you?'

Williams grabbed a flier from the top of the telly and handed it to Scuttle. 'I bung 'em in letter boxes.'

Helen Rochester glanced with a new interest at Williams. 'Thanks, Charlie,' she said.

149

'It says here that you're a carpenter,' Scuttle said.

'Yeah. Well, good as.'

'So you'd own a hammer then?'

Graham Williams looked at Rochester, puzzled. 'A hammer?' Rochester waited. 'Did. Lost it.'

'When?'

Graham Williams shrugged.

'Where, then?'

'Dunno. Could be anywhere. Take your pick.'

'Buy a new one, did you?'

'No.'

'A carpenter without a hammer seems odd. Like a surgeon without a scalpel, wouldn't you say?'

Williams shook his head, 'People don't want nails much no more. And all that hammering ain't necessary no more, neither.'

'When did you last see Ms Tettle?' Rochester asked.

'Last? Only seen her once.'

'Are you sure about that? Not more recently?'

'No.'

'We have a witness who says you did.'

'I never.'

'This witness is absolutely certain. And,' Rochester showed Williams a copy of Brewster's drawing. 'I believe her. Like to think again, Mr Williams?'

A sudden sheen of perspiration glistened on Graham William's forehead. 'Not in her flat, I wasn't. I buzzed, but she didn't answer.'

'So you say that you were not inside the house?'

'No.'

'What did you argue about the first time you called on Ms Tettle?' Scuttle enquired.

The alarm in Williams's eyes confirmed that there had been a argument.

'It wasn't no argument,' he denied vehemently.

'Our witness tells us different.'

Desperation showed on Graham Williams's face. 'I'm a man. She was a woman. Not bad-looking. I thought. . . .' He shrugged. 'You know.'

'No, I don't,' Rochester said sternly. 'So why don't you tell us?'

'Oh, come on.'

'You tried it on,' PC Brian Scuttle stated bluntly.

'No. Told her I fancied her. That we might have some fun. She got uptight. Told me to bugger off, and I—'

'Got nasty?' Scuttle suggested.

'Left,' Williams stated.

'Why did you call round again?' Rochester enquired.

'Short of a fiver, were you?' Scuttle put in sarcastically, much to Helen Rochester's annoyance. Williams was already hostile enough without alienating him further by scoring silly points.

'You're a regular comedian, ain't ya,' Williams said, his mood instantly uglier.

'Answer my question, Mr Williams,' Rochester demanded.

'I was passing. Called to find out if she still needed those doors fixed. Nothing to lose by asking, had I?'

'You took a risk. She might have called the police.'

'Why would she do that?'

'Because Ms Tettle was scared after your first visit?'

'Look, I called round because work is scarce nowadays. That's all.'

'Can't get a reference? It's hard to get one if you struck the foreman in your last job.'

'Been doing your homework, eh,' Williams sneered. 'Yeah. Everywhere I go, that thick bogtrotter O'Sullivan puts in the poison, don't he.'

'I can understand why he'd feel aggrieved. You broke his wrist with a hammer.'

'Pity it wasn't the thick Irish bastard's skull!' said Williams with a bitter anger.

'Like hitting people with hammers, do you?' Rochester asked.

'Don't make a habit of it. The bogtrotter pissed me off. Did time in the nick, but it was worth it.'

'Did Anne Tettle piss you off? Enough to go round to her flat with a hammer, maybe?'

The blood drained from Graham Williams's face. His rat's eyes shot between Scuttle and Rochester. 'What're you up to, eh?'

'You have quite a temper, don't you?' Rochester said. 'You also beat up your cellmate in prison.'

'Self-protection. The bloke I was sharing with wanted me to be Marilyn Monroe to his Cary Grant.'

'A temper that the prison authorities thought you should be treated for at Loston mental hospital, Mr Williams.'

'Depression. You'd be depressed too, if you were in the nick.'

'Do you own a vehicle?'

'Yeah.'

'We'd like to see it.'

'Why? What for? I didn't do nothing.'

'If you didn't do anything, you have nothing to worry about,' Helen Rochester stated.

'Not bloody half, I don't!'

'Just take us to your vehicle,' Scuttle growled.

As they went to the Hiace van that Williams owned, Rochester continued to question him. 'Had your flat repossessed shortly after coming out of Loston mental hospital. Still angry with the manager of the New World Building Society?'

'Carver. That bastard. Yeah, I'm still angry. Wouldn't you be, if he grabbed your gaff? But what's he got to do with—?'

'Caused quite a stir when they opened the new branch of the building society.'

Williams came up short. 'Knew I saw you somewhere before. You were one of the filth who poked your nose in outside the building society.'

'You have quite a flashpoint temper, don't you.'

'You'd be hopping mad, too. When I was in the nick I fell behind. That bastard Carver had me tufted out. Never gave me no chance to make good. Come out of hospital and had nowhere to go. I pleaded with Carver to give me time. I'd have made good on the arrears. But he wouldn't listen. Fucking up his fancy bash was a small compensation. But I'd have preferred to boil the bastard in oil, head first.'

'Still angry with Carver?'

'Not half,' Williams growled.

'Enough to still want to do him a mischief?'

Graham Williams sneered. 'If I live to be a hundred, I'll still want to, as you so politely put it, do him a mischief.' They had arrived at the Hiace van. 'Expecting to find a body in here, are ya?' PC Brian Scuttle sized up the battered Hiace and made a mental note to check its MOT. 'My other motor's a Roller, officer.' Williams sneered, shrewdly reading Scuttle's thoughts.

The van was empty except for a handful of scattered tools and a sheet of black plastic. DC Helen Rochester was about to close the door to go and search the front of the van when she spotted the edge of a darkly stained cloth poking out from under the sheet of black plastic. Using her biro to prevent any contamination of possible forensic evidence, she lifted the edge of the plastic sheeting to reveal the remainder of the cloth, liberally stained with what she was certain was dried blood.

Anne Tettle's blood? Or perhaps Brenda Collins's blood?

'Ever been to a place called Cobley Wood,?' Rochester questioned Williams.

'That's where that hitch-hiker was found murdered. Seen it on the telly.'

'You haven't answered my question.'

'Yeah. I been there.'

'When?'

'A coupla months ago. A picnic.'

Graham Williams did not look the picnic type.

'Forensics will want to look at your van,' she said.

He pointed to the bloodstained cloth. 'Because of that? A virgin.' He laughed cruelly. 'Thirty-two years old and still intact. Bloody amazing, innit?'

'I'll need the woman's name and address.'

'Don't know it. Her motor was broken down. Gave her a
. . . *ride*, as our American friends would say.'

'Where was this?'

'Near Bewley village.'

'Near? Where exactly did you stop to pick up this lady?'

He scoffed. 'Had all the trimmings, but she weren't no
lady. Went at it like a frigging rabbit. Couldn't get enough.
Really put it up to me, I can tell ya.'

'Where?' DC Helen Rochester demanded.

'Don't get your girdle in a twist. 'Bout a mile outside the
village.'

'Going in which direction?'

'What's that got to do with the price of eggs?' Williams
grumbled.

'Answer the question,' PC Scuttle growled.

'Towards Tainside, if you must know.'

'When?' Rochester pressed.

'Day before yesterday.'

'Time?'

' 'Bout eleven o'clock,' Williams groused.

'A.M.?'

'Yeah.'

'You didn't give her a lift, did you?'

'I just—'

'Lied,' Rochester interjected. 'My partner works in
Traffic. He was in a right rant about the backlog of traffic
that built up on the Bewley to Tainside road because of a
jack-knifed truck that completely blocked the road. The

road was closed for four hours, between 10 a.m. and 2 p.m. Now would you care to tell us what really happened?'

'My bloody luck.' Williams groaned. 'OK. I didn't pick her up. I was working for her. Putting up a poxy garden fence. She came out in the garden. I was sitting in my van having my sambos. She sat in. Next thing you know, we were in the back of the van going at it hammer and tongs. I didn't force her. Didn't have to.'

He sneered.

'She tried it once and liked it, right?'

'This woman's address?' Rochester demanded to know.

'Oh, why should I give a toss. She's a big girl.' He took a grubby slip of paper from the pocket of his equally grubby shirt and handed it over to Helen Rochester. 'Thought I might call round again sometime. A bloke's got to provide for a rainy day, know what I mean.'

He winked leerily.

'We'd like you to accompany us to the station, Mr Williams.'

'What for? I've gone bleeding deaf from your questions.'

'It would be best if you came along voluntarily.'

'Was Anne Tettle on your rainy-day list too, Williams?' Scuttle asked.

Graham Williams scowled murderously but did not answer Scuttle's question.

Rochester questioned Williams, 'Who was the woman with you outside the branch of the building society?'

'She wasn't *with* me for starters. Coincidence. She just turned up.'

'So you don't know who she is?'

'Yeah. I know. Her name is Imelda Bell. Carver gave her sister the heave-ho shortly before she was due to retire. Lucy Bell likes her brandy. Got pissed in the office a coupla times. She worked for the building society since the Ark. Imelda Bell was, and is, as angry as a wasp in a bottle 'bout it.' Williams laughed meanly. 'Imelda Bell hates Carver more than me. I got to know Lucy Bell when I went to the branch office a coupla times to try and persuade Carver to give me a chance to make good on my arrears. We went for a drink to a nearby pub a time or two.'

'So you formed an *I hate Jack Carver* club,' Rochester said.

Graham Williams did not deny Rochester's allegation.

Upon returning to the Carver house after interviewing Jen Roberts, DI Sally Speckle was in no mood for nonsense. 'Where exactly is your husband, Mrs Carver?' she demanded to know, and cautioned sternly, 'Witholding information from the police is a very serious matter.'

Flustered, Mel blurted out, 'Brigham. At least that's where he was. Look, Jack is no saint, but he's no murderer.'

'Murderer, Mrs Carver?'

'That hitch-hiker was alive when he left Cobley Wood. Jack told me.' Sally Speckle and Andy Lukeson exchanged glances. A can of worms they had never suspected had been opened. 'It had to be whoever was in the other car, killed her.'

'Other car?'

'A white Almera, Jack said.'

'Did your husband say whether it was a man or a woman in this car?' Lukeson enquired.

157

'It was all fogged up. He could only see a shape.'

'I believe that your husband is into DIY, Mrs Carver?'

'Don't remind me, Sergeant.' Mel Carver groaned. 'I curse the day that I persuaded Jack to do a night course at the local tech. He was always moaning about the dross on telly and I said, well go and do something useful then. Since then there's always someone at the door wanting something fixed.'

'He has a toolkit, then?'

'Oh, not just a toolkit,' Mel snorted. 'Cost a bloody fortune. He's got enough gear in that shed of his to build a skyscraper!'

'Mind if I have a look?' Lukeson asked.

'Please yourself. There's a light switch just inside the door on your left.'

'The key?'

'No key. Just push in the door. A toolkit worth a small fortune, but Jack skimps on a lock for the shed door. Why do you want to see Jack's toolkit, anyway?'

Andy Lukeson ignored the question and made a quick exit from the sitting-room to avoid closer questioning. The garden shed was leaning to one side and seemed in imminent danger of falling apart. Typical, he thought. What was it about DIY enthusiasts and tradesmen (sorry, tradespersons), always doing something for someone else while their own place crumbles round them?

He pushed in the shed door which, as expected, groaned and creaked and stuck on the rough cement floor, forcing Lukeson to lift it up to gain entrance. The light switch matched the rest of the rotting structure. When he flicked the switch sparks flashed from it, which might have had serious consequences. It was not unexpected when the bulb exploded. Luckily, in the splink of light before the bulb shattered, Lukeson spotted Carver's toolkit on a bench to his right. He would have hated to have had to search in the dark. Because in some unidentified place in the shed he could hear rustling.

Lukeson went outside and used the light from the kitchen window to look inside the kit. Jack Carver was a very meticulous man, every tool in its place. Every tool except one, which was missing.

The hammer.

CHAPTER SIXTEEN

Imelda Bell looked closely at the warrant card DC Charlie Johnson was holding up. 'What do you want?' she asked sourly.

'If I could step inside.'

'No need. Say what you have to say and clear off.'

'You are?'

'Good God, don't you know who you've come to talk to?'

'You are Miss Bell, I take it?' He took her lack of response as a positive. 'Imelda or Lucy?'

She waved a letter she had in her hand at him, irritatedly. 'Imelda. Now, again, what is it you want?'

'It really would be better if I stepped inside, Miss Bell,' Charlie Johnson proposed.

Imelda Bell seemed about to reject the idea, but relented. She walked off along the dark, panelled hall. Every inch of the house that he could see had not changed an iota since its Victorian glory days. The furniture was heavy, almost black, with lots of carvings. The walls were bottle-green and the inevitable family figures looked down censoriously from their portraits. The hall floorboards creaked and little puffs of dust rose up with every step – advanced dry rot, Johnson reckoned. Either way, the elderly Imelda Bell and her likewise aged sister would be lucky to die before the house came down around them.

Imelda Bell vanished into a room at the far end of the hall. DC Charlie Johnson had a vivid image of a woman waiting with a poised carving knife when he turned into the room. The strident music from the soundtrack of *Pyscho* filled his head. 'Lost your way?' said Imelda Bell as Johnson held back, amusedly poking her dusty grey head out through the doorway, second guessing Johnson's thoughts.

Johnson was not surprised that entering the room was like walking back into times past. It took no imagination at all to envisage a singer standing by the piano in the mellow glow of candlelight, giving the dinner guests an after-dinner rendition of a popular song of the day.

'Now, young man?' He was thirty-eight. 'Why have you come to bother me?'

'Do you know a Mr Jack Carver, Miss Bell?'

Charlie Johnson was taken aback at the sudden hatred that contorted Imelda Bell's features. She did not need to answer the question. 'Dare I hope that you have brought glad tidings? Has that bastard suffered the most painful and horrible death imaginable?' The look of madness in her narrowed eyes made him swallow hard. In fact, so insanely intense was her gaze that he regretted having come on his own. He checked behind him, just in case Lucy Bell was creeping up on him. 'I was wondering when you'd call.'

'Were you? Why would that be?'

'I knew Carver wouldn't forgo a chance to persecute me,' she said, lemon-bitter. 'But whatever the cost, it was worth messing up the opening of the new branch office of the building society.' Imelda Bell's glinting eyes bore into him. She might be in her late sixties, and not as spritely as she obviously had once been. But the brain behind those eyes was as sharp as that of a woman forty years her junior. 'Lucy gave over thirty years' impeccable service before depression had her seeking consolation in alcohol. Slipped up once or twice. A little too much at lunchtime. Carver had her uncermoniously kicked out with only months to go to retirement. Carver's a vile creature, worthy of extermination for the vermin he is!' Imelda Bell came face to face with Johnson, whose stomach turned at the smell of sour onions on her breath. 'I'll dance a jig on the bastard's grave!'

'Would you say that your sister's feelings are as strong?' Johnson enquired, resisting the urge to turn tail and run.

'No,' said Imelda Bell, critically. 'Lucy is the forgiving type. The stupid *there's some good in everyone* type.' Suddenly all of Imelda Bell's anger dissipated, and was replaced by an overwhelming sadness. 'At least she was.' The quiver of her mouth hinted at tears held back.

'Would it be possible to speak to your sister?' Johnson asked, almost reverentially.

Imelda Bell marched out of the room and up the stairs, leaving Johnson to choose whether he wanted to follow. As he went up the dark, shadowed stairs, the soundtrack from

Pyscho returned. On reaching the landing, Imelda Bell opened a room door silently. 'It's only me, dear,' she said fondly. A woman, who must have been remarkably like Imelda Bell before a stroke had twisted her features, sat looking aimlessly out the window. 'Spends most of her time off somewhere where I can't reach her.'

Imelda Bell's sadness deepened, before anger swept back.

'Jack Carver did that to her!' She turned to face Johnson, her eyes vibrant with hatred.

'Do you know a woman by the name of Anne Tettle, Ms Bell?'

'No.'

'Do you know of Cobley Wood?'

'Yes.'

'When last were you there?'

Recognition flashed in Imelda Bell's button bright eyes. 'Cobley Wood? That's where that hitch-hiker was murdered. Saw it on the news. With Lucy the way she is, looking at telly is about all that's left for me to do now. What has what happened in Cobley Wood to do with me or Lucy?'

'Do you own a car, Miss Bell?'

'No.'

'Can you drive?'

'I don't know. Haven't driven for fifteen years. What's this all about?'

'Just routine enquiries, Ms Bell.'

Suddenly Imelda Bell lost all interest in why Johnson had come. 'Will you be going past the post office?'

'Yes.'

'Good. You can post this letter for me. Biro? Police officers always have biros, don't they?' DC Charlie Johnson handed a biro to Imelda Bell. She took the biro in her right hand and went to a table to address the letter she had been holding. As she wrote the address, the biro slipped from her grasp. Johnson retrieved it and handed it back. She took it in her left hand to complete the address. 'Thanks.' Once outside, he took a couple of deep breaths to clear the smell of sickness from his nostrils, before walking on. Charlie Johnson had not gone far when he stopped dead in his tracks, his mind flashing back to when he had picked up the biro for Imelda Bell. She had used both hands. The right to start with, and the left to finish with.

Imelda Bell was ambidextrous!

The possible significance of that fact crashed in on DC Charlie Johnson. Instinctively, he swung round to look back at the house. Imelda Bell pulled back from an upper window. Had she, as Johnson had, realized her possible gaffe?'

Imelda Bell went to Lucy and gently rubbed her head. Lucy whimpered. 'It's all right, Lucy,' Imelda said quietly. 'Don't upset yourself. Jack Carver will pay for the wrong he did you.'

Perished and starved, Jack Carver looked longingly at the cup of steaming coffee and the baguette which the woman had placed on the dashboard of the Focus before returning to the convenience shop, having obviously forgotten something, leaving the car unlocked. He went towards the car in a meandering stroll. The check-out operator was beginning to be interested in him, the common perception being that shoddily dressed and unshaven equated with thieving. This time, she was right. Carver had every intention of grabbing the hot meal left so invitingly on show. However, when he reached the car and saw the keys in the ignition, he changed his mind. It would be even easier to jump in the car and drive away.

As he sped out of the garage forecourt, Jack Carver thought how easy it was for a man's life to change. Along with being a suspected killer, he was also now a car thief. He would have been caught on the inevitable forecourt CCTV, but what did that matter now?

Where could he go? Mel's sister's place in Devon was out. He could not risk Mel's having been forced to reveal his destination. And for how long could he safely keep driving the Focus? The report of the stolen car was, no doubt, already being flashed to every police car, so the Focus would only be of very limited use.

Feeling faint due to the lack of food, he pulled into a quiet side street and parked between two vans to eat the baguette and drink the coffee before he abandoned the car. 'Nosy old biddy!' he murmured on seeing a twitching lace curtain at a window just outside where he had parked.

Detective Sergeant Andy Lukeson slid DC Helen Rochester's report on Graham Williams across the desk to Sally Speckle. 'Good work,' he commented. 'She'll go a long way, I reckon.'

'Do you think we should have kept Williams in custody?'

'I doubt if we could have,' Lukeson opined. 'There's nothing really definite, is there? Discounting the nicking of a fiver from Anne Tettle.'

'He was at the scene of Tettle's murder,' Speckle said.

'On the street, he claims. And Miss Brewster has admitted that she might have got it wrong and Williams had never actually got into the Cecil Street house. A greenhorn QC would quickly have Brewster in a dither. And he would point out that Williams was one of many on the street. Unless we can definitely place him inside the house. . . .' Lukeson shrugged.

'There's Williams's argument with Tettle.'

'He's not admitting that it was an argument. And Tettle isn't around to contradict him.'

'Miss Brewster said she saw them arguing.'

'A nosy old biddy spying on a young woman in her flat. That's what she'll be seen as by a jury, despite their best efforts to be impartial. And by her friendship with Anne Tettle, it could be argued that she was over-protective of her, or simply biased against a man whom she considered to be a *bad lot*.'

'Well, then, he did attack his foreman with a hammer,' said Speckle, knowing well that Lukeson was correct in how difficult it would have been, even with a reasonably enthusiastic solicitor, to have held Williams.

'He could have attacked half of Loston. But unless we can prove that he attacked Anne Tettle or Brenda Collins, we can't do a thing about it! There's no real proof that Williams is guilty of anything other than being a genuinely dislikable and disreputable lot.'

'You're right, of course,' Speckle said, resigned. 'Even a greenhorn solicitor would have him out in a flash.'

'This woman,' Lukeson said. 'Maybe there's something there we could have Williams for?'

The DI shook her head. 'Checks out. At first the woman denied having sex with a toerag like Williams. What woman wouldn't? But she later relented and verified Williams's story.'

Lukeson shook his head. 'A thirty-two-year-old virgin.'

'I didn't realize that a woman had to surrender her virginity by a certain age,' Speckle shot back, seeing Lukeson's reaction as typically laddish.

The DS was unfazed.

'Still a virgin at thirty-two in these liberated times is, you have to admit, unusual. And Williams's version of how he got involved with her sounds, to say the least, fanciful. Fixing a garden fence and she ended up in the back of his van having sex with him.' Andy Lukeson's tone was sharply sceptical. 'I mean, it's every schoolboy's dream, isn't it. What does this woman do for a living?'

'She's a teacher.'

'Is it likely that a professional woman would find a man like Williams attractive?'

'Helen Rochester says that she's the quiet type. Maybe the floodgates just opened on the spur of the moment. After all, she had bottled up her emotions for a very long time.'

'And maybe it wasn't consensual sex,' Lukeson speculated. 'But, probably, she'll not admit in a million years that Williams raped her, with all that such an accusation entails. The outcome of any rape trial is a throw of the dice.'

'That's how most rapists get away,' Speckle said. 'Women don't want to end up going through hell with nothing to show for it at the end. Anything we can do with Williams's admission that he threatened Carver?'

'He freely admits to that. In fact boasts about it. Carver did cause his apartment to be repossessed. That would piss me off big time,' Lukeson said. 'I'd be angry. I'd make threats. But if everyone who made a threat carried it out, we'd have hospitals full of injured and morgues full of dead.'

'His hatred for Carver is undiminished,' Speckle pointed out.

'I still hate my fourth-form teacher,' Andy Lukeson countered.

'But you wouldn't do him a mischief.'

'If he wasn't seventy-three years old I might smack him one.' Lukeson laughed. 'But knowing Badger Lawson, even at seventy-three, he'd get in first.'

'I don't think we can dismiss Williams, Andy.'

'Until we have our killer, we can't dismiss anyone.'

'I've spoken to the psychiatrist who treated Williams at Loston mental hospital.' Sally Speckle read from her notes. 'Needs anger management therapy. Vengeful. Possibly schizophrenic.' She looked up at Andy Lukeson. 'All ifs and buts, isn't it? And, having admitted that he was in Tettle's flat, any trace evidence that might link him to the scene of the crime will be hotly challenged. Now if we were to find traces of him in Cobley Wood or on Brenda Collins. . . .'

Andy Lukeson frowned. 'Why Collins? What motive?

Tettle he admits to propositioning; a move that obviously backfired. That might have angered him. Helen Rochester says that Williams's temper is never far below the surface. And if he's mentally unstable, her rejection of him might have been the spark to ignite any psychosis in Williams. But why would he kill Collins? And to murder Collins, he had to have followed Carver. Why would he do that?'

'If Williams is psychotic, killing Collins might have made sense to him, Andy.' Lukeson was clearly sceptical. 'Want to hear a crazy theory?'

Lukeson grinned. 'OK. Let's hear a crazy theory.'

'Carver knew Tettle. So let's say that Williams murdered Tettle to drop Carver in it, as a way of getting back at him. Then, for some as yet unknown reason, Williams follows Carver. Carver picks up Collins and Williams can't resist a double whammy.'

'A bit outlandish, isn't it? Murder two women because you hold a grudge?'

'Williams has been in Loston mental hospital. Vengeful and possibly schizophrenic. Maybe it isn't that outlandish an idea after all, Andy?'

'But, again, why follow Carver? Williams could not have known that Carver would pick up a hitch-hiker for him to have, as you say, a double whammy. And how would he have known that Carver was going to Brigham to begin with?'

'I haven't got an answer to your first question,' Speckle said. 'But Williams could have known that Carver was going to Brigham through lmelda Bell. Lucy Bell would have old friends who'd call round. And it's reasonable to assume that Carver would come up in the conversation.'

'And what about Imelda Bell? She could have seen Carver with Tettle. Or seen him go into the Cecil Street house and followed up. Cecil Street is quite close to the Bell house. She could have slipped out and murdered Tettle and be back home again in no time at all.'

'Williams might have fantasized about dropping Carver in it, and Imelda Bell might have acted on it. Of course, it might also be the other way round.'

'Imelda Bell is in her late sixties, Sally. Has no car. How could she have got to Cobley Wood. And why follow Carver?'

'Hired a car?' Speckle ignored the last question.

'To do that she'd need a valid driving licence. She hasn't had one for fifteen years.'

'A friend's car, then.'

'A friend would ask questions. Probably offer to help. And would also probably know that Imelda Bell does not have a driving licence. Would you give her your car?' Lukeson put to Speckle. 'And if she could somehow have got transport, she'd have had to leave her invalid sister in someone's care. That would mean that that person would know that she was missing at the time of Collins's murder, if it ever came to that.'

'You're forgetting that when Imelda Bell would be seeking a car or a minder for Lucy Bell, she would have had no idea that she would end up murdering Collins,' Speckle countered. 'Collins just popped out of the blue.'

'Wouldn't Imelda Bell think – heh, if I murder this woman, someone knows that I'm not at home?'

'If she were rational, yes, Andy. But is she? Obsessed as she obviously is, isn't it feasible to conclude that she might throw all caution to the wind to pursue her twisted revenge against Carver?' Sally Speckle sighed wearily. 'So let's look at what we've got. Williams, Bell and Carver.'

'Working on the idea that Carver is the victim of a sick revenge which, frankly, I'm not too keen to subscribe to,' Lukeson said, 'Bell could have murdered Tettle. But I reckon she could not have got to Cobley Wood to murder Collins.

'Williams is an evil bastard, with a proven violent streak. He could also have murdered Tettle. And he does have transport in which he could have followed Carver. But why he'd want to do so beats me. If the purpose of Tettle's murder was to drop Carver in it, we'd have made the connection between Carver and Tettle sooner or later.

'Then there's Jack Carver. He knew Tettle. Her computer diary clearly links the man who was making a nuisance of himself with the man who fixed her doors – Carver.'

'You're probably right, Andy,' the DI conceded. 'Carver seems to be our best bet.' Sally Speckle frowned thoughtfully. 'Want to hear another crazy theory'? What if Carver and Roberts are lovers? Now Roberts borrows Tettle's laptop and comes across her diary—'

'She'd need Tettle's password.'

'Well, let's assume, for the sake of argument, that she got hold of it,' said Speckle impatiently. 'She might have seen Tettle type it in sometime. Anyway, Roberts reads the diary, sees trouble brewing for Carver and acts to protect him?'

'That's a repeat of the Chambers and Burke scenario.'

'So? Similar situation, similar solution, perhaps?'

'An interesting notion,' Lukeson said. 'Would Roberts act to protect Carver, if she thought he might have tried it on with Tettle?'

'Jealous rage, maybe?'

'Or,' Lukeson said quietly. 'To get her revenge on Carver by killing Tettle? And see him go down for it.'

'So do we actively consider Jen Roberts a suspect, Andy?'

'Maybe there's no harm in putting her on the list. You know, I reckon that when we find out why the killer followed Carver, everything will fall into place.'

Jack Carver was on the last gulp of his coffee when a shadow loomed up at the driver's window. He instinctively knew before he looked up that it was the police.

'Would you step out of the car please, sir?' Carver did as requested, resigned to his fate. 'I'm arresting you for being in possession of a stolen car.' The officer went on to caution him.

The driver of the police car, looking keenly at Jack Carver, got out of the vehicle and had a whispered conversation with his colleague who, in turn, studied Carver.

'Yes, I'm the man every copper in the country must be looking for,' Carver said resignedly, relieved that it was all over. The driver of the police car moved behind Carver. 'How did you find me so soon?'

'You parked in a disabled person's parking space,' said the arresting officer.

Carver recalled the twitching curtain in the house outside which he had parked. 'So bloody simple in the end, eh? I didn't murder those women, you know.'

You'll have a bloody hard time convincing anyone of that, the officers thought. Seeing that during a search of Jack Carver's abandoned Vectra, a bloodstained hammer had been found hidden under the driver's seat.

DC Charlie Johnson burst in the door of Sally Speckle's office. The DI, on the phone, looked at him with annoyance.

'Imelda Bell is ambidextrous. One left-handed killer and one right-handed killer equals one ambidextrous murderer!' he declared.

Charlie Johnson's explanation was unnecessary. Sally Speckle and Andy Lukeson were ahead of him.

'Thanks,' Speckle said and replaced the phone. 'Brigham have just nabbed Jack Carver,' she said.

CHAPTER SEVENTEEN

DI Sally Speckle switched on the tape machine. 'This is an interview with Mr Jack Carver, arrested on suspicion of the murder of Anne Tettle, found murdered in her apartment on Cecil Street in Loston, and a second woman, Brenda Collins, found murdered in Cobley Wood—'

'This is madness!' Jack Carver protested.

'—The time is,' Speckle checked the wall clock in the interview room, 'two thirty-three p.m. Present are DI Sally Speckle, DS Andy Lukeson, PC Robert Archer, the accused Mr Jack Carver and his solicitor, Ms Millicent Scott. The accused has been cautioned.'

Sally Speckle picked up the evidence bag containing the bloodstained hammer found in Carver's car which had been confirmed as the murder weapon in both murders, having on it both Tettle's and Collins's blood, tissue and hair.

'For the benefit of the tape, I am showing Mr Carver the murder weapon. Is this your hammer, Mr Carver?'

'No.'

'You're very sure.'

'It can't be. Bought a new one. The head kept coming off mine. Nearly a nasty accident. I was repairing a kitchen press and the head came off and nearly struck my next door neighbour.'

'That's odd,' Speckle said. 'The head of this hammer is also loose. A bit of a coincidence, don't you think?'

'I don't know what to say,' Carver said.

'Do you still have the old hammer?'

Jack Carver looked at Andy Lukeson. 'No, I don't.'

'Disposed of it, did you?'

'Disposed of, Sergeant?' Millicent Scott questioned. 'That's a rather odd choice of words, wouldn't you say? There is no proof whatsoever that my client disposed of anything, is there? I would ask that a more considerate form of words be used.'

'Where did you dispo— put your old hammer, Mr Carver,' the DS enquired.

'Chucked it in the bin.'

'Do you have a receipt for this new hammer?'

'No.'

'Would you not keep a receipt for a reasonable time, just in case the hammer was not up to spec?'

'What could go wrong with a hammer?'

'The head might come off,' Lukeson said, deadpan. 'What was the name of the store you purchased the hammer from, then?'

'Bought it down the market.'

'And the trader's name?'

'Don't know. Never saw him before.'

'Convenient, that,' Lukeson intoned.

'Traders by their nature are often fly-by-night operators, not given to receipts,' said Carver's lawyer. 'I purchased an electric blanket last winter that functioned for all of three nights. I had no receipt. I dare say that it wouldn't have mattered if I had.'

'There was no hammer in your toolkit, Mr Carver,' Lukeson said. 'New or old.'

Jack Carver looked sheepish. 'I lost it, the new hammer I mean.' Lukeson raised a sceptical eyebrow. 'On my way home from the market I went in for a pint and left it behind in the pub.'

'What pub would that be?'

'The King Charles on Earl Street.'

'Did you check to find out if the hammer had been found?'

'Didn't bother.'

'Why not?'

'Whoever found it would have just walked off with it.'

'Perhaps you did not enquire about the hammer you lost because you didn't lose it in the first place? This new hammer is a fiction concocted by you to enable you to deny ownership of the murder weapon?'

Carver was emphatic. 'I binned the old hammer because it was dangerous, and I purchased a new hammer to replace it which I lost in a pub called the King Charles on Earl Street.'

'So *you* say,' Andy Lukeson scoffed. 'Describe the trader from whom you bought the hammer.'

'Didn't take much notice. Average height. Brown hair, I think—'

'That description would fit half the men in Britain.'

'Well, you don't really look, do you?' Carver complained.

'I would, if I was handing over my cash.'

'You're a police officer. It would be second nature for you to look.'

'Did this mysterious trader have a regional accent?'

'Hard to say. I selected the hammer and handed over the money. He said thanks. That was it. You can't tell much from a single word.'

'OK. Let's recap, shall we? You claim that you purchased a hammer—'

'I did.'

'—from a trader you did not really see, with an accent you can't place. Then you went and lost the hammer in a pub and didn't bother to enquire if it had been found. Do you honestly expect us to believe that load of codswallop?'

'It's what happened.'

'Come on, Carver. I've been down the market. Traders never stop talking. And they're always right in your face, too. I suggest that there was no new hammer,' Lukeson stated emphatically. He grabbed the evidence bag containing the murder weapon and shoved it in Jack Carver's face. 'This is your hammer. The hammer you used to cold-bloodedly and brutally murder Anne Tettle and Brenda Collins.'

'No!'

DI Sally Speckle waited to resume questioning Carver until the tension caused by Andy Lukeson's abrasive questioning eased.

'You again,' Imelda Bell groaned, on seeing DC Charlie

Johnson and WPC Sue Blake on her doorstep. 'What is it now?'

'We'd like you to accompany us to the station, Miss Bell,' Johnson said.

'Don't be daft! Why would I accompany you anywhere?'

'We wish to interview you about the murders of Anne Tettle—'

'Who?'

'—And Brenda Collins,' Johnson said.

'Never heard of either,' Imelda Bell declared.

'We believe that you may be able to help us with our inquiries,' Johnson insisted.

'Well, you believe wrong!'

'I'm afraid we shall have to insist on your accompanying us, Miss Bell,' Johnson said.

'And who'll take care of Lucy?'

'We'll make arrangements for your sister's care during your absence.'

Imelda Bell seemed suddenly to realize the seriousness of her situation. 'Good grief,' she said.

'According to her diary,' Sally Speckle resumed, 'Anne Tettle was contemplating going to the police to report a man who was making a nuisance of himself. She described him as scary. This scary man fixed her doors.' She looked steadily at Carver. 'You fixed doors for Ms Tettle, Mr Carver.'

'Yes, I did. Anne Tettle was having trouble in getting the landlord to live up to his maintenance contract. Jen Roberts, my next door neighbour, who is . . . was a friend of

Anne Tettle, asked me to go round after Tettle had had a bad experience with some man who popped a flier through her letterbox. Rattled her pretty badly.'

Rattled.

The same word Roberts had used to describe Tettle's mood when she had met her at the hospice and had thought that Tettle had had an argument with some man. Speckle shot Lukeson a knowing glance. They were both obviously on the same wavelength.

'Did you phone Anne Tettle at the hospice a short time before she was murdered, Mr Carver?' the DI enquired.

'No. Why would I?'

Lukeson thought that Carver was one of two things, a very good actor or genuinely bemused.

'Had you been phoning Anne Tettle, then?' Speckle asked.

'No.'

The telephone company had had no record of phone calls to Tettle's number from Jack Carver's private number, mobile or office phone. However, there were calls from a payphone to her number, two of which corresponded with dates in Tettle's diary where she had mentioned the man who was making a nuisance of himself. One specifically on the fifteenth of August, when Tettle had used the term *scary* to describe the man. Jack Carver could have been that caller. But there really was no positive way of verifying that he had been. The calls, four in total, had been made from the same payphone, one of the busiest in Loston. So from a forensics point of view it was pretty hopeless. However, it was significant that the payphone concerned was on the corner of the street on which Carver's office was situated.

And it was even more significant that the calls were always made shortly after the building society office closed.

'Or watching her flat?' Speckle enquired.

'No.'

'Did the victim name my client as this man?' Millicent Scott enquired of the DI.

'No.'

'Then this line of questioning is purely speculative and, frankly, close to intimidating, Inspector.'

'There is a definite link made in Ms Tettle's diary between the man who fixed her doors and the man who was bothering her, Ms Scott,' Sally Speckle stated uncompromisingly.

'This is a bloody nightmare,' Carver declared. 'I haven't done anything wrong.'

The interview was interrupted by raised voices in the hall outside the interview room.

'You did it on purpose, didn't you, you cow!' a woman accused.

Sally Speckle looked at Lukeson.

'Don't flatter yourself, you silly bitch!'

Lukeson left to sort out the disturbance.

'DS Andy Lukeson leaving the room at two forty-six p.m.,' Speckle said.

In the hall two WPCs were having a right go at each other.

'Pipe down,' Lukeson ordered them.

'It's her fault, Sarge,' said a WPC he knew as Sarah Sullivan. 'I was on my way to see DS Black. I let a file I had to pass to the DS out of my hand for a second and she hid a photograph of me in a clinch with . . . well, that doesn't matter, in the file. It was at a party and meant nothing.'

'So, what's the problem?' Lukeson asked impatiently.

'Don't you see, Sarge? When I handed over the file and Larry Black opened it, the photograph fell out.'

'Look,' Lukeson said, even more impatiently, 'Am I missing something here?'

'She has the hots for Larry.' Sarah Sullivan pointed an accusing finger at her colleague. 'And she thought by hiding the photograph in the file, she'd drop me in it.'

'Oh, piss off!' said the other WPC. 'Larry is only stringing you along.'

'Shut up, both of you,' Andy Lukeson ordered. 'This is not the time or place to sort out your love lives. Get back to what you're suppose to be doing. Now!'

'You haven't heard the last of this,' Sarah Sullivan warned her colleague, stalking off.

'Shut it!' Lukeson ordered Sullivan, who was about to renew hostilities. 'And I doubt if either of you have heard the last of this.'

Lukeson returned to the interview room and the WPCs went sullenly down the hall.

'DS Andy Lukeson entered the room at two forty-nine p.m.,' Sally Speckle said, obviously seething. 'Sorry about that,' she apologized.'

'Shall I tell you what happened, Carver?' Andy Lukeson said, getting right down to it. 'I think that you tried it on with Anne Tettle—'

'No, I did not,' Jack Carver emphatically denied.

'She rejected you. And, bitter and angry, you began a

181

campaign of intimidation against her—'

'No.'

'Ms Tettle threatened to go to the police—'

'He's talking rubbish,' Carver pleaded with his lawyer.

'And you silenced her,' Lukeson said, as emphatic in his assertion as Carver had been in his denial. 'Still angry, when your plans for Brenda Collins backfired you lashed out again.'

'You can prove all of this, of course, Sergeant?' Millicent Scott asked. 'No? Then no more fanciful speculation, please.'

'Brenda Collins was alive when I left her at Cobley Wood,' Carver stated. 'She got out of the car to spend a penny and took an age to return. I was caught for time, and by then anyway I knew that I had been very stupid. As I drove off I saw her in the rearview mirror.' Desperately, he claimed. 'Someone is trying to frame me for murder.'

'Frame you for murder? Lukeson scoffed. 'Oh, come on.'

'I think you should let my client say what he has to say, Sergeant,' Scott said.

'Go on, Mr Carver,' Speckle said, drawing a scornful look from Andy Lukeson.

'There was a car,' Jack Carver said. 'It was parked under some low-hanging trees, nearer to the entrance to the wood. A white Almera.'

'Did you see who was in this car?' Speckle asked.

'It was fogged up. I could only see a shape.'

'What was your impression then? Male or female?'

Conscious of Mattie Clark's possible presence in the wood, Carver said, 'Could have been be a woman.'

'Did you get the car's registration number?'

'No, Inspector.'

'If, as you are claiming, someone is trying to frame you for murder, do you know anyone who owns a white Almera?'

'Yes,' Jack Carver said quietly, knowing well the can of worms his admission would open up. 'A colleague.'

'Name?'

'Mattie Clark. Matilda Clark. She was right behind me when I turned into the Coach and Four pub. Almost a pile-up. A black Ka behind her had the devil's own job to stay on the road. She might have stopped at Cobley Wood.'

'Why would she do that?' Speckle asked.

'She might have wanted to talk about something. We are colleagues, after all.'

'Talk?' Lukeson said. 'A close friend, is she? Maybe even a very close friend?' Jack Carver cast his gaze down. 'This close friend. How might she react if she saw you with Brenda Collins?'

'I don't know.'

'Badly?' Lukeson suggested.

Carver shrugged.

'What exactly is your relationship with Clark?' Speckle enquired.

'We're . . .'

'Lovers?'

Jack Carver's demeanour made it unncessary for him to answer the question.

'Then it's reasonable to assume that Ms Clark may very well have reacted badly, wouldn't you say, Inspector?' said

Millicent Scott, quick to try and shift the blame from her client.

'Mattie – Ms Clark would have had nothing to react badly to,' Carver said, much to the annoyance of his solicitor.

'What exactly would Ms Clark have seen, had she been there?' Sally Speckle pressed.

'Nothing much.'

'Can you be more precise, Mr Carver?'

'We had a bit of a clinch,' Carver admitted. 'Lasted only a second. Brenda Collins had to pee.'

'How intense is your relationship with Ms Clark?' Lukeson asked.

'Fun and games kind of thing,' Carver said.

'Fun and games. Does Ms Clark see your relationship in the same way?'

Jack Carver averted his gaze from Andy Lukeson's intense scrutiny. 'She wants me to leave my wife.'

'Poacher wants to turn gamekeeper, eh?'

'Do you and Ms Clark work together?' Speckle questioned.

'Not in the same office, no. She's from up north.'

'North? But if she was coming from the north she wouldn't be anyway near the Loston to Brigham road.'

'Down visiting a sick friend in London, she said.'

'And the name of this friend?'

'She didn't say.'

'Well we can always get an officer from Brigham to ask her,' Lukeson said.

'Do you have to?' Carver pleaded. 'Right now Mattie Clark has a bee in her bonnet about me leaving Mel, my wife. The police popping up won't make it any easier.'

Sally Speckle was unsympathetic and reminded Carver that, being the chief suspect for the brutal murder of two women, upsetting his lover was the least of his worries. 'This is a murder inquiry, Mr Carver, and you have introduced Ms Clark as a possible suspect. Did you make Ms Clark aware of Anne Tettle?'

'You make it sound like there was something going on between Anne Tettle and me. All I did was repair her doors.'

'If she knew, perhaps Ms Clark thought there was more to it? And you didn't answer my question.'

'I might have said something. I can't really say. Mattie Clark and I were not into small talk.'

'Did she say when she left London?'

'No. Does it matter?'

'Maybe it does,' Speckle said. 'You see, Ms Clark may have been in Loston when Anne Tettle was murdered.'

'Is that all you've got?' Imelda Bell's solicitor asked DC Charlie Johnson. 'Is this whole interview based on the fact that my client is ambidextrous? Have you a single shred of proof that Miss Bell even knew the victims? And this idea that she would commit murder as a form of revenge against this . . .' he checked his notes '. . . Carver, is risible.

'We have two murders,' Johnson said. 'The first victim, we believe, was murdered by a left-handed killer. While the second victim was most definitely murdered by a right-handed killer. Therefore, I'm sure you can readily understand our interest in a possible suspect who is

185

ambidextrous, Mr Wallingford.'

'Believe?' Wallingford pounced. Charlie Johnson cursed silently at having, by his careless use of language, allowed for a doubt that Wallingford could and would exploit. 'You said you believe the first victim was murdered by a left-handed killer. Aren't you sure?'

'As far as we can be,' Charlie Johnson answered lamely.

'*As far as we can be,*' Wallingford intoned. 'It's my experience that these matters can be proved or discounted very early and very quickly, DC Johnson. Obviously not in this case. So I put it to you that this exercise is simply a fishing expedition and should be immediately abandoned to avoid a possible action for wrongful arrest. This débâcle is causing undue stress and anxiety to Miss Bell, and I would advise that this charade be ended forthwith.'

WPC Sue Blake shifted uneasily. Such a disaster as Imelda Bell's lawyer alluded to would not be good early in her career. Of course hers would only be a very minor role in the affair, a bit part, but mud stuck. When her hope that Charlie Johnson would be steered towards caution by Wallingford's remarks, vanished, Sue Blake wished that she could slip under the door and be gone.

'Miss Bell lives quite near to where the first victim, Ms Tettle, lived,' he said.

'Oh, dear me,' Wallingford scoffed, with the air of a victor. 'Is living near someone now a good enough reason to be accused of murder? And the second murder, in Cobley Wood? What fanciful reason can you put forward for that, eh, DC Johnson? Miss Bell does not have a car, and hasn't driven for a very long time. In fact she does not have a driving licence. My understanding is that the police believe that Ms Collins was murdered by Carver or someone who followed this fellow Carver and was purely an opportunistic act of violence. Is that so?'

'It's one line of investigation,' Charlie Johnson replied, by now sinking without trace under Wallingford's heavy fire.

'So, without a car, Miss Bell would have had to rely on public transport. And, as far as I am aware, public transport runs to a timetable and cannot be ordered up on a whim to suit one's . . .' his sarcasm reached its most virulent '. . . murderous intentions, DC Johnson.'

Let that be an end of it, Sue Blake prayed. How many warning shots across his bows did Johnson need?

'Would you be willing to co-operate in providing your fingerprints, Miss Bell?' Sue Blake thought she would faint. 'And allow a DNA sample to be taken?' The room spun for Blake.

Imelda Bell held up her hand to stay Wallingford's outraged protest. 'Why not?' she said. 'If it will clear up this silliness.'

'Look,' There was a new degree of desperation in Jack Carver's voice, 'there was this bloke in the pub who tried to pick up Brenda Collins. He was really pissed off when he lost out. He could easily have followed us and—'

'We know of him, Mr Carver,' Speckle said. 'And we have ruled him out.'

'Why?'

'Because at the time Brenda Collins was murdered he was in police custody. He had an accident shortly after leaving the Coach and Four pub and was arrested for being over the legal limit.'

Sally Speckle wondered how the interview had gone from one of tying up loose ends to the consideration of another possible suspect in this Clark woman. Imelda Bell being ambidextrous was of interest, of course. However, there was a stack of damning evidence against Carver. Clark was a flier. They had their man and it was time to stop the nonsense and charge Carver. Sally Speckle was about to do that when Helen Rochester entered the room.

'DC Helen Rochester has entered the room at three twenty-five p.m.,' said Speckle, for the benefit of the tape. Rochester handed Speckle a computer printout and left immediately. 'DC Rochester has left the room at three twenty-six p.m.' She read the printout and was more certain than ever that the man sitting across the table from her, one Jack Carver, was guilty of the murders he was accused of committing. She passed the printout to Lukeson and waited until he came up to speed. Then:

'How do you feel about lesbians, Mr Carver?' she asked.

'Lesbians? You mean do I hate them?'

'*Hate.* A very strong word – hate.'

'You're attempting to read something in to my client's reply that is not there, Inspector,' Millicent Scott intervened.

'Am I, Ms Scott? Your client used the word hate, not me. So do you hate lesbians, Mr Carver?'

'No.'

'Exactly what are your feelings towards the gay community?

Having had a gay brother who had succumbed to Aids, DI Sally Speckle felt uneasy with the line of questioning. One terrible memory surfaced, of answering her doorbell one night to find her brother slouched outside, bruised and bloodied, after a couple of so-called men had decided to, as he had told her, straighten him out. She studied Jack Carver, trying to see any hint of homophobia, before realizing that some of the most heinous crimes had been committed by perfectly ordinary, in fact often affable and charming, people. There was no way to see inside the dark recesses of a poisoned mind.

'Live and let live, I say,' Carver said.

'Did you know that Anne Tettle was a lesbian?'

'Yes.'

'Did she tell you?'

'No.'

'Then how—?'

'Instinct. Well, you know these things, don't you? You get a feeling about them, if you're straight.'

'Does the name Alice Wingard mean anything to you?' the DI asked.

'Alice Wingard?' Carver shook his head.

'Sure?'

'Yes.'

'Alice Wingard is the name of a woman you assaulted in Edinburgh in 1982 – October the tenth, to be precise. Do you want the time of the assault?'

Millicent Scott shot Carver an alarmed look.

'I'd forgotten.'

'Forgotten? You assaulted a woman and you'd forgotten?

Not something you'd forget, is it? Unless, of course, you thought little of the assault, Alice Wingard being a lesbian. In fact you might have thought that being a lesbian, she was fair game for a red-blooded male.'

'I was in the army. Nineteen years old and bloody brutalized by a sergeant-major who would have been considered to be a bad lot in a Nazi death camp. I was stressed out and went AWOL. Next thing I know, the police are on my doorstep telling me that I assaulted a woman. It was the first I had heard of it. I had suffered stress amnesia. The army medics confirmed that.'

'Was this a sexual assault, Inspector?' Scott enquired.

'No, it wasn't,' Jack Carver said. 'It was nothing more than a slap in the face.'

'Oh, more than that,' Speckle said. 'The woman suffered a facial laceration.'

'A nick under her eye,' Carver said.

'A long way from murder, Inspector,' his lawyer said, off balance after what amounted to a bomb being dropped.

'Obviously the army had its concerns, Mr Carver,' Sally Speckle said. 'They discharged you.'

'I'd have slapped someone earlier if I thought it would have got me out of the army! The military life and I were simply incompatible. I didn't know that she was quee— gay.'

'Oh,' Andy Lukeson exclaimed. 'What about those instincts you have? You told us just now that you instinctively knew that Anne Tettle was a lesbian. Yet you didn't know that Alice Wingard was?'

'I . . . I . . . Well, I wasn't myself, was I?'

190

'Come on, Carver,' Lukeson scoffed. 'You knew Alice Wingard was a lesbian, and that was why you smacked her.'

'No. How could I know that someone I had just met was gay?'

'Instinct? Maybe all this about instinct is just rubbish. And you only discovered Anne Tettle was gay when you tried it on.'

'I didn't touch her.'

'Really,' Millicent Scott protested. 'Have you any evidence that my client, as you put it, *tried it on*, Sergeant?'

'I think my sergeant's interpretation of what might have happened, based on the contents of Ms Tettle's diary is reasonable, Ms Scott,' Speckle said. 'In it she mentioned being bothered by a man. The man who fixed her doors.'

'Anne Tettle was living alone, gay, in a strange place. Probably deeply unhappy. Isolated. Under such circumstances, it isn't unknown for lonely women to fantasize.'

'Lonely Ms Tettle might have been. But no one has suggested that she was delusional, Ms Scott. On the contrary, she seems to have been a very well-balanced and level-headed person.'

'Take your opportunities, do you, Carver?' Andy Lukeson asked.

'Inspector,' Scott protested vigorously, smarting from Sally Speckle's no-holds barred response. 'I really have to object. Such intemperate language from your sergeant is an unambiguous attempt to portray my client in a most unfavourable light.'

'Well, that's what you were doing when you picked up

Brenda Collins, wasn't it?' Lukeson said, ignoring the lawyer's protest. 'Taking an opportunity.'

'She picked me up.'

'You expect us to believe that?'

'It's what happened.'

'What did your instincts tell you about Brenda Collins?' Andy Lukeson enquired. 'Was she gay?'

'Definitely not. She was on the game.'

'A working girl who perhaps privately might have had other preferences. Know women well, do you?'

'I'm not claiming to be a saint,' Carver admitted.

'So you do take your opportunities, then?'

'Not that again,' Carver's lawyer complained. 'What relevance does this line of questioning have?' she quizzed Speckle.

'Do you, Carver?' Lukeson persisted, doggedly. 'Take your opportunities? And if one does not present itself, do you create an opportunity, perhaps?'

'Don't be daft. Look, when are you going to listen to me. Someone else did this to—'

'Frame you,' Lukeson intoned tiredly. 'We know.'

'It makes sense to me,' Jack Carver stated. 'Because I know I did not murder anyone.'

'Who, other than Ms Clark, might this mysterious person be?' Speckle enquired.

Jack Carver offered Graham Williams and Lucy Bell as possible culprits.

'Lucy Bell is an invalid, Carver,' Lukeson said. 'Stroke.'

'Her whacky sister, then. She made threats to get even with me after I gave Lucy the push. I even considered going to the police. And Williams is a vicious bastard. Said a hundred times that he'd get even with me.'

'Imelda Bell is a woman in her late sixties,' Speckle said. 'She doesn't have a car. Hasn't held a driver's licence for fifteen years. She also has to nurse her sister constantly. Even had she murdered Anne Tettle in Loston, getting to Cobley Wood to murder Brenda Collins would be a problem.'

'She could have hired a car.'

'She'd have needed a valid driving licence to do that.'

'A friend's car, then.'

'Possible. But a friend would probably ask why she needed the car and where she was going. And that would be letting someone in on a secret that Imelda Bell would want to keep. And, of course, she would have to get someone to sit with her sister. That would be one more who would know that Imelda Bell was somwhere else at the time Brenda Collins was murdered. Not the ideal preparation for murder, is it?'

'But she wouldn't be planning murder when she set out, would she? 'Carver pointed out. 'Because she could not have known that I'd pick . . . befriend . . . Brenda Collins.' It was a valid point. A very valid point indeed. 'But why would she follow me?'

Prompted by the argument between the WPCs in which he had intervened a short time before, a possible answer to Jack Carver's question flashed to Andy Lukeson's mind. If, as WPC Sarah Sullivan claimed, her colleague had hidden a photograph in a file to drop her in it, then might the mysterious killer who, Carver claimed, was framing him, not have done the same by hiding the murder weapon in Carver's car? And it explained how Brenda Collins became a victim, too.

'Did you lock your car when you went into the pub?' Lukeson enquired of Carver.

'Yes. I'm very careful about that. Had a car nicked once in seconds.'

'Was there any time when you left your car unlocked?'

DI Sally Speckle wondered about the purpose of Andy Lukeson's questions. What had Carver having locked his car to do with anything?

'No.'

'Sure about that?'

'Yes. Positive.'

Andy Lukeson was flummoxed.

Making a mental note to ask her sergeant about his line of questioning, Sally Speckle took up the initiative again.

'Can you explain how your fingerprints were found on a drinking glass in Ms Tettle's flat?'

'Anne Tettle offered me a drink when I fixed her doors.'

'When was this?'

'A couple of weeks ago.'

'You can't seriously be offering that as an explanation,' Speckle scoffed. 'All the evidence points to Anne Tettle being a very neat and precise person. She'd hardly leave a glass unwashed for weeks. You'll have to do better than that.'

'Your prints were also found on the flap of the pocket of Ms Collins's rucksack, Mr Carver.'

Jack Carver shifted uneasily. Admitting to how his

fingerprints had got on Brenda Collins's rucksack would not help him.

'Well, Mr Carver?' Speckle insisted.

'I, ah . . . Well. . . .'

'Yes.'

'You might say that, not having received what I'd paid for, I reckoned no play no pay was reasonable.' He said nothing about stealing another hundred pounds from Collins.

'Let me sum up for you, Mr Carver,' the DI said. 'The weapon used to bludgeon Anne Tettle and Brenda Collins was found hidden in your car. Your fingerprints are on it, and only your fingerprints. And your prints were found at both murder scenes. Your blood is on Brenda Collins's jeans—'

'I can explain that. I was in a hurry to be away from the pub. My hand slipped on the handbrake and I grazed it. 'See,' he held up the knuckles of his left hand for examination. 'I pulled my hand away and it brushed against her jeans.'

'In Anne Tettle's diary there's mention of a man who had fixed some doors for her making a nuisance of himself,' Speckle went on. 'In fact "scary" was how she described this man. You fixed Anne Tettle's doors. And you picked up Brenda Collins, and took her to Cobley Wood for sex. Shortly after she was also found bludgeoned to death by the same hammer that was used to murder Anne Tettle. Blood, tissue and hair samples substantiate this. And I have every confidence that the trace evidence at the scenes will further implicate you in these women's deaths.'

Panicked, Jack Carver looked to Millicent Scott for reassurance. Her return gaze held little hope.

'You're absolutely certain that you locked your car at all times?'

What was Lukeson's preoccupation with whether Carver's car was locked or not? Speckle wondered, irritably.

'Yes,' Carver confirmed. 'I never . . . The service station near Cobley Wood,' he exclaimed. 'The pumps were on the blink. I left the car unlocked while I used the loo. I remember trying to figure out how raindrops had got on the driver's seat, because the window was closed. Obviously it was when the killer opened the door to hide the hammer! The killer followed me because he wanted to hide the murder weapon in my car. The murder weapon found in my car would damn me to hell, wouldn't it? Clever bastard!'

The murder weapon found in Carver's car would most assuredly make a powerful impression on a jury. But wasn't there also the chance that Jack Carver was this very clever bastard he spoke of? He could have purposely held on to the murder weapon to lend credence to the idea that he was the victim of this mysterious enemy out to get him, should he need to. A short time before he had pondered on why the killer had followed him. And now he recalled that he had left his car unlocked, timely so, perhaps? Had he cleverly led them by the nose to where he wanted them to go? Was Jack Carver that devious? Would he have been so stupid as to hide the murder weapon in his car? would be the question uppermost in a jury's mind. And one that would be exploited to the full by his defence should he end up in the dock.

'Inspector,' Millicent Scott's tone was one of utter weariness, 'Mr Carver is exhausted. I suggest a rest period is in order.'

Sally Speckle thought about charging Carver, but she had the distinct impression that Lukeson would prefer an intermission rather than a final curtain. 'We'll resume in an hour.'

'I rather think that an hour is too little,' Millicent Scott said.

'One hour, Ms Scott,' Sally Speckle stated resolutely. 'Interview suspended at four twelve p.m. Well, what do you think of all that?' she immediately enquired of Andy Lukeson when PC Archer led Carver and his lawyer away.

'I think you were wise to hold back on charging him,' Lukeson opined.

'You do? Chief Superintendent Doyle might not agree. There's a lot of evidence.'

'Never hurts to give yourself a breathing space to sit and think things through. Nothing worse than having to withdraw a charge. And there's also the possibility then of a civil action.'

'And how did you get on to the idea that the supposed killer followed Carver to hide the murder weapon in his car, Andy?'

Lukeson explained where the idea had come from. And also his thinking on how clever Jack Carver might have been, should he be caught. 'And he could have another string to his defensive bow, Sally.'

'Like?'

'Acting while under amnesia brought on by stress.'

'Oh, come on, Andy. I reckon that that whole episode was a clever ploy by Carver to get himself kicked out of the army. And even if by some remote chance it had happened, Carver would have had lots of stress since. So that brings up the question of why now would he suffer amnesia?'

'That may be so. But he's got the army medics on his side. And you know how impressed a jury might be by such evidence. And in the hurly-burly of a courtroom, with competing experts for the prosecution and defence, it's a toss of the coin, isn't it? And he can point to a lot going on in his life. A tough time at work and a mistress putting the squeeze on him. Lots of stress there. Carver could be aiming for a plea of diminished responsibility, should he need it.'

'OK. If Carver was thinking along those lines, wouldn't he have admitted to the Alice Wingard episode to bolster any such defence? He had acted violently once, why not again?'

'Wouldn't want to seem too eager? Better to let it evolve. If it hadn't, he could always get a sudden flashback.'

'Like he did about his car?'

'Like he did about his car, indeed,' Lukeson said. 'And he may also have been clever enough to leave all that evidence lying around at the crime scenes on purpose. After all, a man acting in the throes of amnesia would hardly be aware of it, would he? And, of course, the other side of the coin is that, having left all that evidence, he might very well have acted during a genuine bout of amnesia.'

'I don't believe that for a second, Andy.'

'And, of course, Carver could be telling the truth, also. Maybe the killer did follow him to hide the hammer in his car.'

PC Brian Scuttle breezed into the interview room to declare: 'We've got Carver on CCTV at the off-licence on Cecil Street at the time Anne Tettle was murdered. Puts him right there at the scene of the crime.'

CHAPTER EIGHTEEN

'There's something I want to talk to you about, Jen.'

'Talk to me about?' Roberts enquired curiously. 'Sounds serious, Mel.' Roberts stepped aside. 'Well, you'd better come in then, hadn't you.' She ushered Mel Carver into the sitting-room. 'I'll bring a cuppa. Must just pop upstairs first. Got some lovely coconut cake. My sister Sara's recipe.'

A short time earlier, passing a photograph of her husband taken a couple of years previously, Mel Carver had come up short, inexplicably uneasy. Frank Crowther's earlier phone call had echoed in her mind. *'Jack and I did a stint in Saudi Arabia.'* Her mouth, as dry as Saudi sand, Mel took the photograph from its frame, fetched a pencil, and with a trembling hand she had added a beard to her husband's image, and staggered back.

Mel now took the doctored photograph from her cardigan pocket where she had put it before leaving home a few moments ago; a picture taken five years previously on a trip to Cornwall on a day of brilliant sunshine and Mediterranean temperatures. In it, Carver had his arm round Mel's shoulders, hugging her to him. And were she to vanish from the photograph, to be replaced by the woman Jack had been hugging in the group photograph in Arthur Granger's album from his time in Saudi Arabia, the picture would be a carbon copy of the Granger photograph.

Jennifer Roberts arrived back with a tray, placed it on the coffee table and sat opposite Mel. 'Well, then,' she said cheerily. 'Tell Aunty Jen why you're so glum, Mel. Isn't this continuous rain awful. It's almost dark already.'

DI Sally Speckle came grimly downstairs from her meeting with Chief Superintendent Doyle. 'Let's have Carver in again, Andy.'

'Sermon acting up, is he?' Lukeson asked, studying his superior's grim expression as they walked along the hall to the interview room.

'I take it you mean Chief Superintendent Doyle,' she snapped. 'Well, he wants to know why I didn't bang Carver up. He also wants to know how the overtime budget is twenty per cent over. And I'm not sure to which complaint he allots more importance. And I'm sorry for biting your head off, Andy.'

They turned into interview room three.

'Well, Jen,' Mel Carver began. 'You know how sometimes something that you feel should have made sense, suddenly, like a bolt out of the blue, does?'

201

'Yes. So what came to you like a bolt out of the blue?'

'Well—'

'Oh, by the way, Mel. I'll be moving. To a little hamlet in Norfolk. My sister Sara's cottage. After she died I wasn't ready to move in. I had so much to think about then. Sara was a really good soul. As well as being my sister, she was my best friend. Loved her to bits, really, 'Jen Roberts said wistfully. 'I had things to do. Now it's time to claim my inheritance.'

Her laughter was infectious.

'*Claim my inheritance*. God, it sounds like a line from a BBC costume drama. All it's lacking is a loving *'Papa'*. It's all a bit sudden, I know. But the lease on the cottage is up more or less at the same time as the lease here is.'

Jen Roberts poured the tea.

'Better have this before it goes cold. I hate cold tea.' She placed a plate of coconut cake between them on the coffee table. 'Drink up, then.'

'I'll be sorry to see you go, Jen.'

'Will you?' Jen Roberts's gaze had come to rest on the photograph Mel was holding, unwittingly turned towards Roberts by her fidgeting fingers. 'I doubt that very much, Mel.'

DI Sally Speckle switched on the tape machine in interview room three. 'DI Sally Speckle. The interviewing of Mr Jack Carver is resuming. Also present are DS Lukeson, Ms Millicent Scott, Mr Carver's lawyer and PC Robert Archer. The time is five thirty-two p.m.

'It has come to our attention, Mr Carver, that you were

present in Cecil Street at six forty-five p.m. on the evening of Anne Tettle's murder.'

'So? I was at the off-licence there, getting wine for a friend's wedding anniversary party.'

'Did you visit Ms Tettle's flat when you were there?'

'No.'

'There's an off-licence in Crew Square, just round the corner from Allworth Avenue where you live, Mr Carver. Why didn't you go there? Why go all the way to Cecil Street for an off-licence when there was one on your doorstep?'

'Simple, Inspector. There was a two-for-one offer at the Cecil Street off-licence. I had a gift voucher to cash in, which my next door neighbour had given me when I would not accept payment for some DIY work I did for her.'

'That would be Ms Roberts?'

'Yes.'

'Came in handy, this voucher,' Andy Lukeson observed. 'Gave you a reason for being on Cecil Street at the time Anne Tettle was murdered.'

'Pure coincidence.'

'Inspector, my client is under a great deal of stress which, from past experience, we know that in Mr Carver's case can have dramatically adverse effects on his well-being and personality. I refer, of course, to the Alice Wingard affair.'

Sally Speckle and Andy Lukeson exchanged glances. Lukeson thought that if he ever needed a solicitor, he'd want Millicent Scott in his corner. She had obviously used the break in the interview well – very well indeed.

'What are you suggesting, Ms Scott?' Sally Speckle enquired stiffly.

'Ms Tettle was a lesbian. And so, in the absence of proof positive, that may also have been Ms Collins's true nature. The human mind often reacts in a sinister manner when a combination of factors which previously triggered a specific response are repeated.'

Raising Jack Carver's assault on Alice Wingard had always been a double-edged sword. It was proof of Carver's violent reaction to a lesbian. However, it had also left the door open for a clever lawyer like Millicent Scott to put forward, as she had done, a defence of diminished responsibility based on repeated circumstances evoking a repeated response. A clever defence QC could go a long way in sowing doubt in a jury's mind.

'Is this what you're claiming happened, Mr Carver'? Speckle asked.

'I suppose . . . Well . . . Oh, bloody hell!' He addressed his solicitor. 'Look, I appreciate what you're trying to do, Ms Scott. But the fact of the matter is that I have perfect recollection of events, and I didn't murder anyone.'

'My advice would be—'

'I know what your advice would be,' Carver interjected. 'But like I said, I didn't do anything. So why should I spend even a single day in prison?'

'The mind is a strange thing,' Scott argued, valiantly trying to regain lost ground.

'I told you,' Carver exploded. 'I have perfect recall. And, I repeat, I did not murder anyone!'

Millicent Scott's shoulders slumped.

Sally Speckle's feelings were mixed. As things stood there were sufficient grounds to charge Jack Carver with murder, plain and simple. However, Carver's fiery rejection of his solicitor's strategy of *diminished responsibility*, and his insistence that he was not a murderer, troubled her. Were Carver guilty, would he not have grasped the opportunity to face a judge and jury on such a plea? The fact that he had not, made Jack Carver one of two things, Speckle thought – a fool or, disturbingly, an innocent man. But, in the final analysis, she was a police officer with those *sufficient grounds*, and therefore it was up to her to do her job and a defence and prosecution to do theirs – a judge to direct, and a jury to consider.

'Mr Jack Carver, I am charging you with the murders of Anne Tettle and Brenda Collins. Anything you say may . . .' As she recited the caution, Sally Speckle's voice, to her, seemed to come from a long way off, unnerved as she was by her first charge of murder, the outcome of which would decide her entire career.

Would it be DI Sally Speckle, hero? Or would it be DI Sally Speckle, clown?

CHAPTER NINETEEN

Andy Lukeson was in the canteen drinking a cup of mysterious black liquid which he had been assured was coffee when DC Helen Rochester and a rookie she had taken under her wing joined him. 'Sally Cross, Andy Lukeson.'

Lukeson shook the rookie's hand and Cross grimaced. She rolled up her sleeve to reveal a crêpe bandage.

'Sprained my wrist, a bloody nuisance. My left hand is useless. Weak as a newborn kitten.'

Andy Lukeson sat upright as if someone had plugged in his chair to the electric socket. His mind raced back to a visit to Jen Roberts with Rochester, when the DC had sat on a novel and a crêpe bandage. Had Roberts also sprained her right wrist? Might that explain the weak and multiple left handed blows to Tettle.

'You saw a Labatt's bag with a tracksuit in it, in Roberts sitting-room, didn't you?' he quizzed Rochester.

'I wondered about that,' Rochester said. 'She certainly doesn't need to jog. And by her own admission she hates exercise. So why a tracksuit, Sarge?'

'I think I know why,' Lukeson said. 'Can you recall what the tracksuit looked like?'

'Yes. It was pretty distinctive. It had a red stripe with a wavy yellow line running through it.'

'So you'd recognize the make if you saw one again?'

'Yeah.'

He took three ten pound notes from his pocket and handed them over to Helen Rochester. 'That should be enough.'

Rochester giggled. 'Enough?' She put on airs and graces. 'I'm not your every day slapper, guv.'

Before she laughed, Sally Cross checked Andy Lukeson's reaction.

'Go round to Labatt's and buy a track suit exactly the same as the one you saw in Roberts's sitting-room. And while you're doing that get someone to check with the car-hire companies. Find out if Roberts hired a car – probably a black Ka.'

'Roberts has a car of her own, a red Fiesta.'

'A car that would be readily recognizable to anyone who knew Roberts. Go!' Lukeson hurried from the canteen, punching out the number of Loston Hospice on his mobile. 'Mrs Gerrard,' he demanded.

'Who will I say is calling?'

'DS Lukeson. Loston CID.'

'She is rather busy at the moment, Sergeant,' said the voice on the other end, obviously hoping that he would accept the answer and just go away.

'Tell her that it's urgent police business,' he barked.

'Perhaps if I ask her to call you back?'

'Do you understand the meaning of urgent?' Lukeson growled.

After a moment, Gerrard came on the line.

'What is it you want, Sergeant?' she enquired, making no effort to hide her annoyance.

'Can you recall what Ms Roberts was wearing on the evening Anne Tettle was murdered, Mrs Gerrard?'

'I thought this was urgent police business, Sergeant,' she answered, huffily. 'It seems to me—'

'Can you recall?' Lukeson interjected. 'It is important.'

'Yes. It was most unsuitable attire. Normally Jen Roberts is rather well turned out. Frankly, she's not the tracksuit type.'

Lukeson's fist punched the air.

'Was she carrying anything?'

'Some shopping.'

'What kind of shopping?'

'Clothes, presumably, seeing that it was a Labatt's shopping bag.'

'And finally, is Mrs Clancy's room, the patient Roberts sat with, on the ground floor? And does it have a view of the hospice entrance?'

'Both. But I can't see what releva—'

'You've been most helpful, Mrs Gerrard.'

'Have I? I can't see how, Sergeant.'

He sought out Sally Speckle, who had gone to Sermon Doyle's office to inform him that she had charged Jack

Carver with murder.

'If you wouldn't mind excusing us for a moment, sir,' he said. 'It is important.'

'Too important for my ears, is it, Sergeant?' Doyle asked sourly. 'I think we're about finished anyway, Inspector. I'll arrange a press conference right away to announce that we've charged Carver.'

'What is it, Andy?' Speckle asked immediately on leaving Doyle's office. 'Couldn't it have waited for another couple of minutes?'

'I think we've cocked up.'

Speckle's step faltered. 'Cocked up?' The blood drained from her face.

'I reckon that Jack Carver did not murder anyone. I think I know who did. And how it was done.'

'Oh, shit!'

She sagged against the wall, Doyle's voice ringing in her ears.' *I'll arrange a press conference right away to announce that we've charged Carver.*

'I'd better. . . .' She looked behind her at Doyle's office door with trepidation. 'Shit!'

'Don't be silly. Of course I'll miss you, Jen,' Mel Carver said. 'We've been good friends.'

'Yes, we have, haven't we?' Jen Roberts mood was reflective. 'Pity you made the connection between Jack and Arthur Granger, Mel. I sensed you had the second I opened the front door to you.'

'I don't know what you're talking about. Connection? What connection?'

'Tut tut, Mel. It's right there in your hand.' Mel Carver had not realized that her nervous, fumbling fingers had turned the altered photograph of her husband towards Jen Roberts.

Roberts pulled a face. 'I used to do that when I was a child, add beards and moustaches to faces to see what difference it would make.' Leaning forward, she grabbed the photograph from Mel Carver and studied it. 'A beard doesn't suit Jack. Makes him look . . . well, thuggish.'

She was suddenly angry.

'But, of course, that's what Jack Carver is, Mel – a thug! What prompted you? The group photograph, was it? You gave no hint. At the time, I wondered if I'd done the right thing, discussing that photograph with you.'

'Nothing to do with the photograph, not then anyway. A phone call from one of Jack's old friends,' Mel said, 'whom he hadn't seen for a long time. He asked me if Jack still had a beard.'

'As simple as that. Did you never feel anything, living with Jack?'

'What do you mean?'

'Jack's a murderer, Mel. He murdered my sister. He's a rotten, deceitful, lying bastard.'

'Murdered your sister?' Mel exclaimed, breathless with shock.

'Oh, yes. Jack and Sara the woman he's hugging were an item back then, in Saudi Arabia. He got Sara pregnant and then did a runner, leaving her holding the baby, literally.'

Jen Roberts sighed.

'I've never been a lucky person. But this time I was

certain my luck had changed. I thought that the bastard who murdered my sister would finally pay for his crime!'

A dark and dreadful thought sprang to Mel Carver's mind. 'How do you mean? Pay for his crime?' Then with a flash of clarity, she knew that her dark thoughts were right and horror took her over. 'You murdered those women to get back at Jack, didn't you?'

'I thought Doyle would blow a gasket,' Sally Speckle said, mounting the steps to Henrietta Brewster's front door. 'But when I told him we knew who the killer was, he calmed down. Now I just hope that there's not another cruel twist to all of this, Andy.'

Lukeson's mobile rang just as he knocked on Brewster's door.

'Brian Scuttle, Sarge. Roberts did hire a car. A black Ka.'

'Who are you?' Henrietta Brewster demanded to know of Lukeson through the partly open front doors.

Sally Speckle leaned forward. 'Hello, Miss Brewster.'

'Inspector,' she enthused, immediately throwing open the door. 'So lovely to see you again so soon, m'dear.'

'This is my colleague, Detective Sergeant Lukeson.'

Lukeson took from his pocket the photograph he had taken from Jen Roberts to repair. Luckily, he had put it in his locker to wait until he got round to getting it reframed. He showed the photograph to Miss Brewster.

'That's her,' Miss Brewster exclaimed immediately. 'The woman who dumped that rubbish in the river. The jogger I told you about, Inspector.'

'Sure?' Lukeson asked.

'Certain. I hope you're going to summons her for littering, are you?'

'Now one more thing.' Lukeson took the tracksuit that Helen Rochester had purchased from a Labatt's shopping bag. He held it up for Henrietta Brewster's inspection. 'Is this what the woman was wearing, Miss Brewster?'

'Yes. It's exactly the same, Sergeant.'

'You've been most helpful, Miss Brewster,' Speckle said.

'I had a stroke of good fortune, Mel. When Anne Tettle told me she had some doors to fix, it came to me in a flash. I'd send Jack around. Then I'd murder Anne and set Jack up for it. Jack deserves to rot in prison for life, Mel,' Roberts said matter-of-factly.

'But why?'

'Why?' she said angrily. 'That's bloody obvious, you stupid cow. When Jack took off, Sara was shattered. She came home to Norfolk. Brooded a great deal. I tried to persuade her to have an abortion, but Sara was old-school Catholic, you see. That's why I never suspected that she would harm herself. But she did. Hanged herself.

'I tried to find the man who had destroyed Sara's life. I'd never met him, you see. Never even seen a photograph of him. They had only been going out together for a couple of months. Then one day I visited Arthur Granger. He was reading the *Loston Echo*. "I know that bastard," he said, showing me a picture of a group outside the opening of a new building society branch in Loston. He was pointing at Jack.

'He asked me to take an old photograph album from his bedside locker and showed me the group photograph. "That's Carver," he said, pointing to the bearded man with an arm round Sara. 'You can imagine my shock, Mel. "Got her pregnant and did a runner. I'd have married her in a flash," he said. "But she wouldn't have me. Didn't think it was fair to off-load Carver's bastard on me. But I wouldn't have minded," Arthur said. "I loved her."

'Arthur wept then.

' "Sara was her name," he said, "I worshipped the ground she walked on." He went on to tell me about Sara's suicide, while I sat there quietly seething. Imagine, I was living right next door to the man who had so cruelly betrayed my sister.

'I could hardly breathe, Mel. From that moment on, there was only one thought in my head. And that was to avenge Sara's death. To make Jack belatedly pay the price for murder. Those women would still be alive, only for Jack,' she said with the vagueness of one drifting into another place. 'They died because of Jack's wrongdoing. I had to make Jack pay, can't you understand that? He had to rot in prison!'

Her anger was suddenly terrifying.

'And now you've ruined everything!'

'You're insane. I'm phoning the police.' Mel stood up and wobbled. The room spun.

'Just a couple of sleeping pills kicking in, Mel.' Jen Roberts stood up and grabbed her. Mel looked into Jen Roberts's evil, distorted face. 'I'll give you the rest of the bottle when I get you home.'

213

She laughed mockingly.

'You just couldn't take all the stress you've been under, Mel. People will understand.'

Mel Carver tried to fight Roberts off, but darkness was closing in on her.

DS Andy Lukeson turned in to Allworth Avenue. He pulled in and parked under a stout oak between Roberts's and Carver's houses. He was getting out of the car when he saw Jen Roberts making her way round the side of the Carver house, Mel Carver leaning on her and teetering drunkenly. 'Hold it right there,' he commanded. Jen Roberts stopped dead in her tracks. 'The game's up, Roberts.'

Jen Roberts looked with a furious madness at Andy Lukeson before going completely limp. She dropped Mel Carver on the ground.

'She didn't understand. But I'm sure you will, Sergeant. Shall we go inside?'

'Yes. I think that would be best.'

'I'll request an ambulance,' Speckle said.

'What put you on to me, Sergeant?' Jen Roberts asked, once inside.

'A rookie with a sprained wrist.'

'The crêpe bandage that DC Rochester sat on, right?'

'Yes.'

'It's always something simple, isn't it.'

'You sprained your right wrist and had to use your left hand, your weaker hand to inflict the blows on Anne Tettle, didn't you?'

'It was very awkward. The bitch nearly got the upper hand, you know.'

'Then I began to wonder why someone who doesn't need to jog, who in fact by her own admission hates exercise, needed a tracksuit.'

'I saw DC Rochester looking at the tracksuit in the Labatt's shopping bag I had left so carelessly on view. I should have got rid of it, but it was new.'

'The Sylvia Murray factor,' Lukeson said.

'Sylvia Murray?'

'Oh, nothing.'

'Do go on, Sergeant, I'm quite intrigued.'

'You bought two identical tracksuits. One tracksuit to wear going to the hospice, and to wear while you murdered Anne Tettle.'

'Quite a messy business, bludgeoning.'

'And a second, identical tracksuit, to return to the hospice in to make it look as though you had never left.'

'How very clever you are, Sergeant. Please go on.'

'You went to the hospice to discuss rejoining Mrs Gerrard's adopt a patient scheme with the intention of sitting with Mrs Clancy, terminally ill and heavily sedated and, most important, occupying a ground-floor room; she was perfect. The room gave a view of the hospice entrance, and when you saw Anne Tettle leave, you slipped out the window and ran ahead to reach Tettle's flat before her. You murdered Tettle, changed track suits, and then on your way back to the hospice dumped the bloodstained tracksuit in the river, from where we no doubt will retrieve it.

'You then returned to the hospice and Mrs Clancy's room

the way you had left. You phoned Mrs Gerrard to express your concern about Mrs Clancy's supposed restlessness, knowing well Gerrard's addiction to *Coronation Street*. You knew, of course that she would send someone along to check on Mrs Clancy, and Nurse Walsh's attendance and your phone call to Gerrard gave you what appeared to be an airtight alibi.'

Jen Roberts was smiling smugly.

'Clever, wasn't I? Even if the smelly old biddy woke up, hopped up to her eyeballs as she was she might as well have been on another planet. Someone might have come in while I was off beating Anne Tettle's skull in, but it was a small risk. I could say that I'd gone to the loo.'

'How did you get in to the Cecil Street house?'

'I have an excellent memory. One evening I waited until Anne came home and popped up behind her when she was punching in the access code. Simple.'

'And the key to Tettle's flat?'

'That was easy. Anne was always losing or misplacing her key. One day last week, said I was passing and just popped in to say hello. Took the key out of Anne's purse while she made coffee.'

'She might have changed the lock.'

'If Anne had to replace the lock every time she lost her key, I don't think the manufacturers could keep up the supply. Idiot that she was,' she laughed contemptuously. 'I stole another key, too, but that didn't work out as well.'

'From the Carvers?'

'Yes.'

'You needed the key to Jack Carver's car to hide the

murder weapon in it, didn't you?'

'You really should be top of the class, Sergeant,' Roberts said, with genuine admiration.

'So, why didn't you just pop the murder weapon into Jack Carver's car after killing Anne Tettle? Why follow him to do it?'

'Simple. The key I stole from Mel was her sister's, who had been visiting and left it behind. So, not being able to open Jack Carver's car, I had to follow him. Car hire is so expensive these days,' she complained. 'Even for a small car like a Ka. An expense I could have done without, I can tell you, Sergeant. But, you see, I couldn't risk using my own car to follow Jack, he'd have spotted me, wouldn't he?

'And it all worked out for the best. A bloody murder weapon found in his car would have made quite an impression on a jury. I was lucky that Jack stopped for petrol. The pumps were on the blink. Jack is meticulous about locking his car, but he left it unlocked for a minute while he used the station loo. So I popped the hammer under the driver's seat.

'Think about it, Sergeant. If I had got the right key to Carver's car, that other woman need not have died.' She said it as if Brenda Collins's murder had been just a silly and inconsequential event. 'But it was an opportunity too good to miss, really.

'I hung around outside the pub Jack had gone into to follow him again. I saw him come out with the woman, and the reason he was with her soon became obvious. She was a dirty, filthy whore!' Roberts screamed. 'And Jack was with her!'

'You were in love with Jack Carver, weren't you? That's what this is all about. The revenge of a jilted lover.'

'Don't talk nonsense. It was just a silly summer evening thing that happened for no good reason other than that we both had had too much to drink. Jack was quick to set me straight.' Jen Roberts glared at Andy Lukeson with hateful intensity. But then the hate and anger vanished, and were replaced by overwhelming defeat and sadness. 'Like I was telling Mel. I never was a lucky person.' She frowned. 'How could you have known that I dumped the blood-stained tracksuit in the river?' she asked curiously. 'The river path was absolutely deserted.'

'A birdwatcher with a pair of binoculars a couple of streets away saw you.'

'There again, rotten luck.' She looked vaguely at Lukeson, as if she were slipping into some unknown place. 'The computer was a nice touch, don't you think? I thought the mysterious HE was quite inventive. Then the tie-up between HE and the man who had fixed Anne's doors was, if I may say so, rather brilliant.

'Anne, the stupid cow, just handed over her laptop to me when I spun her a silly story about wanting to write a novel.'

'How did you get Ms Tettle's password?'

'Oh, I came up with a cock and bull story about a friend of mine not being able to recollect her password. Some Russian word that she had completely forgotten. Anne said it was best to keep it simple, like a pet's name, something like that.

'I knew that she had had a pet cat in London that she'd

been very attached to, and it had died. Tiddles. All too easy, really. You think people would give a little more thought to what they say and do in these identity-theft times.'

'You're not as careful when you think you're talking to a friend,' said Andy Lukeson, pointedly.

'I've always found that a friend is the last person you should trust, Sergeant.' Jen Roberts sighed wearily. 'The jilted lover, eh? Do you know why I did all of this? Jack Carver murdered my sister Sara, and he had to rot in jail.'

'Murdered your sister?'

'As good as.' Jen Roberts told him about her fateful visit to Arthur Granger. 'Life's a funny old thing, isn't it,' she said wistfully. 'Imagine. If the New World Building Society had not opened a new office in Loston, I'd have never found the man who was responsible for my sister's death, and two women would not have needed to die.

'From the second I knew that Jack Carver was the man who had been responsible for my sister's suicide I planned to revenge Sara's death. But how? That was my dilemma. Then fate took a hand. One evening Jack Carver was repairing a kitchen press. I was having a cuppa with Mel. The head flew off the hammer he was using and it almost hit me. Jack slung the hammer in the bin. Later that night I popped round and retrieved it. At the time I wasn't sure why I did, but the plot to make Carver suffer for his misdeeds must have been bubbling away in my subconscious, I suppose. Because later that night I woke from sleep and, hey presto, I knew exactly how I was going to do it. By arranging for him to be convicted for murder he'd rot in prison.'

'You murdered two innocent women,' Lukeson said sternly.

'You can't make an omelette without breaking eggs, eh, Sergeant?' she said, matter-of-factly.

She's as mad as they come, Lukeson thought.

'Don't you see? It was all Jack Carver's fault. If he hadn't done what he did, then there would have been no need to punish him. And I had to make it convincing, didn't I?'

She laughed in a little-girlish way.

'I'd need . . . *things*. Things that the police would find and match. A couple of hairs from his hair brush, easily obtained on a visit to the Carvers' loo, to put on Anne's body later. A drinking glass with his fingerprints on when he and Mel came round to dinner. And I had to make it look as though Jack Carver was making a nuisance of himself to Anne. Hence the doctoring of Anne's computer diary.

'Scene set, I left my phone number by Anne's bedside to lead you to my door. I needed the police to find me, so that when you read Anne's computer diary where the man who had fixed her doors and HE were linked, I'd be able to tell you that it was I who had sent Jack Carver round to her flat.

'And wasn't that gift voucher to the off-licence on Cecil Street a stroke of genius? Mel told me that a friend's wedding anniversary was coming up and, Jack being a penny-pinching bastard, I knew he'd never be able to resist the off-licence's two-for-one offer. The offer was only on between 5 p.m. and 7 p.m. on the night. It put him right at the scene of the crime, and close to the time I murdered

Anne Tettle. As a matter of fact, I watched him go by on the street from Anne's flat.

'It was such a perfect plan. And,' she said excitedly, 'those phone calls I made from the payphone near Jack's office to Anne Tettle. I knew you'd check on any calls to her number to try and pin-point the man who was scaring her. Didn't say a word. Just phoned and then hung up. But I had every confidence that when the police checked, the link between the calls from the payphone near Jack Carver's office, each call made about the same time, just after the building society office closed, would tighten the noose round Carver's neck even more than it already had been.'

Jen Roberts maniacal laughter faded away. DS Andy Lukeson nodded to a WPC, who came and led Jen Roberts away. 'Before you go . . .' Roberts paused in the doorway. 'How did you manage to preserve Carver's fingerprints on the murder weapon so perfectly?'

'Simple. I used my own hammer, which you'll find in the attic, to commit the murders. I was careful when I retrieved Jack's hammer from the bin to use a rubber glove to pick it up by the head. Then, later, I dipped the head of Jack's hammer in the gore to get all that lovely evidence. I never touched the handle of the hammer. Sometimes, the simple things work beautifully, don't you think?'

She turned to leave, but turned back again.

'What made you think I changed my tracksuit, Sergeant?' she asked.

'Oh, that idea came from a chatroom romance.'

'You must explain sometime, Sergeant. I'm very tired

now.' She laughed sadly. 'I almost got away with it, didn't I?'

'Almost,' Lukeson conceded.

'Do give Jack my very best, won't you?'

'Under arrest,' Graham Williams scowled. 'What for?'

'We've spoken to the woman who you said was a willing partner, Williams . . .' DC Helen Rochester let the sentence hang in the air unfinished, hoping that the bluff Andy Lukeson had contrived would work. 'The art of suggesting that you have more than you actually have often works,' Lukeson had advised her. And, seeing the colour drain from Graham Williams's face, Rochester reckoned that the strategy might very well be working.

'Cow!' Williams exploded furiously. 'She was asking for it. Wearing crotch-hugging jeans like that.'

'You did good work, Andy,' Sally Speckle said, sipping her G&T.

'We *both* did good work, Sally. Like I said, police work is a team effort.'

Andy Lukeson's mobile phone rang.

'It's worked, Sarge,' Helen Rochester crowed over the air waves. 'Williams has admitted to rape.'

'Don't jump too high, Helen,' he cautioned. 'The woman still has to admit she was raped and bring charges, which she probably won't do. But at least, in the meantime, Williams will sweat a great deal.'

'Could I have a word, guv?' Sally Speckle looked up at PC Roger Bennett. 'Alone.'

'Excuse me, Andy,' she said and went to join Bennett, who had moved away to a quiet corner of the Plodders Well. 'You were Jeff Hornby's line into the inquiry, weren't you?' Speckle shrewdly guessed.

'Yes. Owed money to some nasty types. Slow horses.'

'Have you a gambling problem?'

'I think I might have, ma'am.'

'Then, if you like, I'll arrange for someone you can talk to.'

'You're very kind. What about. . . ?'

'Disciplinary procedures? Let's see how things work out first. OK? Thanks for coming forward.'

'Last orders!' the landlord of the Plodders Well shouted, just as Sally Speckle arrived back.

'Another?' Andy Lukeson asked.

'I don't think so. I've got to get home.'

'I'll see you home.'

'Will you? Well, in that case, I'd love another drink, Andy. Do you like Mozart?'

'Wasn't he a guitarist with The Police?' Lukeson said, tongue in cheek. 'Or was it—?'

'I just want to warn you that I always play Mozart when I'm tipsy.'

'And when you're drunk?'

'I think I'm Maria Callas.'

'Oh, doesn't matter.'

'Doesn't it?'

'No. When I get pissed I get this crazy notion that I'm a detective.'

'Maybe we should just have a coke?'

'Oh, what the heck!' Andy Lukeson grinned. 'I'll be Pavarotti to your Callas.' His grin widened. 'I might even play the saxophone.' He shrugged. 'Well, try to, anyway. But somehow the notes just keep changing round all the time.'

Speckle laughed.

'Just like clues, Andy. Just like clues.'